The Paddle Club

A fun, romantic and erotic spanking novel

Susan Kohler

CCB Publishing
British Columbia, Canada

The Paddle Club: A fun, romantic and erotic spanking novel

Copyright ©2007 by Susan Kohler
ISBN-10   0-9781162-7-5
ISBN-13   978-0-9781162-7-9
First Edition

Library and Archives Canada Cataloguing in Publication

Kohler, Susan, 1950-
The Paddle Club: A fun, romantic and erotic spanking novel / written
by Susan Kohler. – 1st ed.
Also available in electronic format.
ISBN 978-0-9781162-7-9
I. Title.
PS3611.O47P33 2007   813'.6   C2007-903695-3

Publisher: CCB Publishing
             British Columbia, Canada
             www.ccbpublishing.com

Dedication

This is to the people out there who love spanking, and especially to two spanking groups in my area filled with wonderful, lively and intelligent people. I love you guys. You are the best. You do more for me than I can ever say. I'll admit some of you are featured in this book, but relax; I kept your identities protected. Of course, if you want to brag, go ahead.

Other books coming soon by Susan Kohler

Hot Crossed Buns

Another Batch of Hot Buns

Both books contain collections of short spanking stories.

For more information please refer to
Author's Note on page 221.

Preface

This novel starts with a fairly graphic caning scene. The scene follows the path of many spanking novels out there: The girl being caned is young and anonymous. She is being caned against her will, victimized and humiliated. It is the only such scene in this novel and is an example of what I wanted to get away from.

My characters are not victims. They enjoy spanking. They are also not all young girls. They are adult women and men, of various shapes and ages. Many switch from top to bottom. I really like these people. They have fun and they like to party.

Most of what I've written, I've seen and done. With two exceptions: We don't have initiations, and I've never been in a slave auction.

Contents

Chapter One

What Do You Wear To Be Caned?

Suzanne was both disgusted and captivated as she turned the page and read:

The girl stood stock still, petrified. She was barely eighteen with a slender body, moist blue eyes and long blond hair pulled back at her neck. She stared at the rod held so lovingly, so menacingly, in the headmaster's hands and shivered.

Finally the quiet, dreadful command came. "Take off your skirt, Miss, fold it neatly, and place it on that chair."

When the skirt had been folded and placed on the nearby armchair, he spoke again, his voice louder and lower pitched. "Please remove your panties. I want to punish you on your bare bottom. It's the only way to punish you properly. It will hurt you more and also humiliate you."

She lowered her panties to the floor. She stood there, shivering in the cool room, immobile and embarrassed. She was suddenly aware of the open study window and of the furtive faces looking in. Male faces, filled with lust. She was being watched! A blush crept up her neck to her face.

"Put them on the chair, folded neatly." His voice was gruff. He pointed at the sofa. "Kindly bend over girl. Right over the end of the sofa, with those legs spread well apart. Let's get this shameful business over with as soon as possible. I hate this onerous duty but I'm forced to whip you into obedience, to beat the defiance out of you."

Her legs trembling, she moved to comply. For several long moments, she lay there. At his urging, she squirmed, trying to get into the position he wanted. Finally he moved her forcibly; bending her more tightly over the padded end of the sofa so that her bottom was raised well up and her legs far apart. Her toes barely touched the floor. Her pale bottom was a perfect, heart-shaped target. It was also positioned so that anyone looking in the window could see every detail.

The master stoked her behind gently before he raised the rod, drawing it well back before slashing it down on her with a terrific cut. She gasped with the pain but she made no outcry. The whipping continued, she wiggled and squirmed as cut after cut landed on her soft, exposed bottom. Her gasps became screams. Welts crisscrossed her tender flesh, and droplets of blood appeared on her skin. Her screams combined with sobs. She kicked out with her feet. He slashed viciously with the rod, using an upstroke, bringing it up under her bottom. He slashed to the tops of her thighs. Then he slashed down on the crests of her buttocks. She squirmed and screamed more and more.

"Hold still girl and cease that noise or I'll add another dozen cuts!" he said sternly. "Surely you can take a little punishment better than that!"

She tried, really she did, but eventually she moved to cover her bottom with her hands. It was exactly what the master wanted! He quickly moved to grab her hands in one of his and gave her six quick slashing cuts as hard as he could!

When it was finished, she lay there, defeated and spent. Her quiet sobs filled the room. The master walked over to draw the drapes. He returned to the sobbing girl. He was now gentle as he stroked her soft bottom, tracing the welts and spreading the small drops of blood over her tender, bruised flesh. Eventually she heard the sigh of a zipper and soon realized that it was not his hands stroking her soft flesh. Not daring to move, not even daring to breathe she waited, tense and uncertain as she felt his hands spreading her flesh, urging her rear cheeks apart. The tip of his...

Suzanne sighed and threw the paperback across the room. It hit the wall with a soft thud and fell to the floor. She lay back on the bed and slid her hands down, her fingers parting the soft folds of her flesh, working gently but furiously to bring herself some relief even as she felt dirty and disgusted for reading the book.

Later, as she lay on the bed, she wondered how those girls always managed to hold themselves in position, only wiggling and squirming enough to earn extra strokes. Why didn't they kick? Get off the bench or sofa and fight back? Run? They were also so damned compliant before the whipping started. They stood still, removed their clothes in front of the man who was going to whip them, with an audience no less, and then meekly got into position for their whipping. No struggling and no protesting.

Well, she felt as if she wouldn't have any chance to struggle or protest either, in her upcoming spanking. She would be forced to comply. She would be stripped in front of an audience and strapped down when she finally found out how a cane really felt. The very thought put her into a haze. In fact, she had been in an emotional haze all day. She teetered back and forth between wondering how she had gotten herself into this situation, secret arousal and excitement, and complete denial that anything was going to happen. How could she have agreed to it? How could she have let her lover talk her into going to an S & M club? Was she nuts?

The feelings only sharpened while she was dressing and getting ready for her evening out with her lover, Michael. He had made the plans. Plans she had agreed to with a lot of reluctance and great deal of trepidation, and quite a bit of secret excitement.

Still, there was something so unreal about the evening ahead of her that it almost felt as if she was getting dressed to play a part in a movie, a very exotic and somehow erotic foreign film. She felt almost like a puppet being manipulated against her will, and yet that wasn't quite right. She had given her agreement freely, hadn't she? But why? She wasn't really sure.

It wasn't just to shut him up, to stop his constant alternation between commanding and pleading; she silently answered her mental question. She had agreed because agreeing to the date was her last attempt to hold onto a failing relationship and out of the same rather mindless curiosity that killed the proverbial cat.

Michael's plans for the evening began with her initiation into a club for spanking enthusiasts. She looked in the mirror and ruefully shook her head, grinning sardonically at her reflection. Spanking. What was she thinking?

Spanking was something she had never tried before, something she had read about in books like the one tossed across the room and secretly fantasized about, but never really thought about trying before she met Michael. In fact, she had never previously been spanked by any of her boyfriends, even by her parents. In all her twenty-five years, Suzanne had never been so nervous or so aroused.

In plain English, she was dressing up to be publicly stripped naked then caned and paddled. She shuttered and put the palms of both hands over her bottom, imagining her buttocks were already bruised and the blood had already started to flow. That's morbid, she thought, there won't be any blood, not really.

Going to the club was strictly Michael's idea. Something he pushed Suzanne into doing, threatening to end the relationship if she refused. Something, he had said with a smirk, which was sure to add a bit of spice to their sinking relationship. The whole evening was one more of Suzanne's attempts to do anything to please Michael, and it was certainly more than she felt he deserved. Lately he had become arrogant and demanding, also very mean-spirited. The only reason she had agreed to this evening's plan was because she was intrigued and slightly curious about spanking, and by the thought that such a club even existed. What kind of people were in the club and what could they possibly be like?

Of course there was also the poignant memory of how sweet Michael had been when they first started to date, before he seemed to change. There was another reason she agreed to go to the initiation, a reason that she had not yet admitted, even to herself.

Suzanne sat on the edge of the bed and remembered her first date with Michael as she pulled the black lace stockings up her long, slender legs fastening them with her garter belt. They had gone to a very expensive, five-star restaurant near the marina and following the superb meal, walked along the beach talking and holding hands. Michael was funny and kind. He was older than Suzanne, ten years older, but he was slender and fit. He had a kind, almost boyish quality. That date, the first of many, ended with a gentle kiss.

She put on a black lace bra and stood as she pulled on a pair of matching panties, pulling them up over her garter belt. Sitting down on the bed again, she continued her mental replay of her relationship with Michael. She remembered how his optimistic outlook disappeared when he lost his job through no fault of his own. He had been blamed for another man's incompetence.

As he searched for a new job his hostility grew until, by the time he finally found a position his whole personality had completely changed. It got even worse once he was working again at a more menial job; his deep bitterness was mixed with a fierce and hard-hearted determination to move up the corporate ladder. The combination of bitter ruthlessness and fear of failing had completely robbed him of the simple joys in life.

Even their dates had changed; there were no more simple walks along the beach or picnics in the park. Now all their dates were business related social functions. Michael liked having a poised and polished Suzanne on his arm at these affairs. He thinks of me almost like he does his expensive watch or his gold signet ring, Suzanne realized, as though I'm an expensive status symbol. A trophy girlfriend. How did I ever let him get away with that kind of behavior? She wondered, disgusted with herself.

Suzanne then pulled on her dress, a sexy but very modest piece of blue satin that was not very tight but clung to her slender waist and hugged her well-rounded buttocks and her large, firm breasts. The dress was not especially low cut, but it was still in some ways, very lush and sensuous.

The color brought out the vibrant blue of her eyes. Her long, straight, shiny black hair was piled on top of her head, and she wore no make-up except blush to emphasize her high cheekbones and lipstick to bring out her full, perfect lips.

She was ready. One more time she sat on the bed and thought about Michael. She hoped against all hope that her willing participation tonight would show him that they still had a relationship worth saving. Extremely nervous and very frightened, she almost felt like an old-fashioned bride on her wedding night, facing the unknown for the first time. She looked very sensuous and at the same time, elegant. Her height, at 5'9" was tall enough to give her an almost queenly air in the silky formal gown.

In spite of her nerves, her natural grace and poise added to the total picture of regal serenity. She had a bearing of gentility and maturity that completely masked her lustful nature and her wicked sense of humor.

Smiling to herself she remembered the first long phone call she had received from a member of the club. The man, who had identified himself as James, was the club's host for the initiation. His voice was exceptionally kind and his manner surprisingly reassuring.

James told her about the club, and explained about tops and bottoms. He told her that for some reason their club had an unusually high percentage of members who would switch from one to the other; he called it going from topping to bottoming. The members were generally monogamists, not into wild orgies, and he explained that nothing would happen to her against her will. He gently spelled out what would happen at the club's initiation, and gave her explicit instructions on what she was to wear and how to act.

He gave her code words to use if she wanted things to stop or just to slow down, and told her the code words were for her protection. She should challenge herself to avoid using them, if at all possible, but to shout them out when she felt she needed to. No one would think the less of her. He also assured her that there would be no blood and she would suffer no real injuries.

He made sure she had no illusions or hidden surprises waiting for her at the club's initiation but told her that her lover,

Michael, would indeed be on the receiving end of a surprise, a big one. The surprise was almost the last thing James told her as he explained the club to her. His explanation was strangely reassuring.

James concluded the call by recommending a couple of erotic books featuring S & M and by saying, "Don't get so nervous, it'll be fun, a little scary maybe and a little painful certainly, but still fun. Not at all like those books." He laughed softly, "I'll bet you even like most of the people in the club. We really aren't as weird as you probably think we are. Remember, I'll be there to make it just as good as I can for you, okay?"

James told her most of the details about the surprise they had in store for Michael. If his voice and manner hadn't been so warm and courteous and even somehow strangely reassuring in spite of the very painful plans he had in store for her, Suzanne probably would have backed out of the whole affair. Even though she hadn't realized it, James was the third reason she had agreed to go to the club. Even over the phone, he intrigued her.

Michael, ever the perfectionist, arrived precisely at eight o'clock. He used his own key to let himself in, and walked up the stairs and right into Suzanne's bedroom. Suzanne turned to study him. He had become a stocky man, now about thirty-five. He looked out of his element standing there in his tuxedo. In spite of a spare tire beginning to form around his waist he was still a fairly attractive man. His boyish charm had vanished, leaving behind a man who was handsome in a dark, brooding sort of way. He had an aquiline face, with short, dark brown hair, brown eyes and thin lips. He hid the bitter aspects of his nature under a facade of expansive good humor.

Since his gradual transformation into a mean-spirited and merciless man, his favorite hobby was criticizing and baiting Suzanne. He seemed almost disappointed that she was ready and waiting for him, and that she had followed his instructions perfectly. She had left nothing for him to criticize, and that was the worst sin of all. He vowed to make her pay and had the perfect means to torment her. Just to irritate Suzanne, Michael had her pull up her dress and look at her own ass in the full-length mirror.

"Take a good look at that pale butt before the club members get their hands on it. It's going to be so red and hot, I can hardly wait. I bet it will hurt like hell. In fact, if I close my eyes and use my imagination I can almost see the welts right here." He put his hand on her ass and he taunted her cruelly, with no hint of his former affection.

Suzanne wondered to herself why she didn't just dump this loser, but almost against her will she found herself walking down the stairs with him. When they got outside she noticed a long, white limousine waiting for them.

"The club sent it to pick me up," Michael boasted. Big shot!

"It's picking me up, too, Michael," Suzanne muttered under her breath.

The limo driver turned out to be a kindly looking older man about sixty. He was short and chubby. He had merry green eyes and wavy, snow white hair. The man introduced himself as Jerry and said he was a member. He held the door very formally as they got into the car. As Suzanne got in he gave her a lusty swat on the left cheek of her buttocks. Even through the dress the swat made her bottom sting and tingle.

"Sorry, Miss. I got ahead of myself." He sounded completely unrepentant then laughed at the surprise on her face, and winked. "Maybe later you can pay me back for my dreadful impertinence."

She sank back into the plush velvet interior of the limo. Michael got in beside her. The upholstery was burgundy and the rest of the interior was rich wood paneling with gold trim. The limo was fully stocked. It had a small bar with champagne and tall, crystal fluted goblets. There was a television, a phone and a small drawer filled with condoms. In addition to the champagne, a shelf above the bar had a bottle labeled "Spanking After Care Lotion" on it. The sight of the lotion and the thought of its possible use made Suzanne's mouth feel dry. During the ride to the club headquarters her butt tingled on the spot where the cheerful chauffeur had slapped it.

When they arrived at the club Suzanne had a brief glimpse of a large brick building, with white trim. There was a covered porch that ran the whole length of the front of the building. It was also painted a gleaming white. There were several wrought iron chairs and wooden swings on the porch, and a well-manicured lawn surrounding the long, curving driveway. The gardens in front of the porch were planted with colorful flowers, mainly roses, and there was a trim hedge around the property. The limo let Suzanne and Michael out before it pulled right into a large, enclosed garage.

Several club members came out of the clubhouse to greet the new couple. Suzanne noticed immediately that they were a very diverse group. She saw people of all ages, from early twenties to late sixties, and all sizes from thin to fat, mixed racially between White and Hispanic. Were there any members of the other races, Blacks or Asians, she wondered vaguely in a corner of her consciousness, or does a club like this practice racial discrimination?

Suzanne relaxed a little as she realized that the members all seemed to be very friendly and normal, even ordinary. Most of them acted very cheerful and welcoming. Secretly she was glad to see that none of the members present were wearing any weird black leather outfits, with shiny silver studs or carrying whips.

A stranger seeing the group would think they were gathered for an elegant ball since they were all dressed formally in lovely evening gowns and well-tailored tuxedos complete with white tie and in some cases, even tails. As the group moved into the clubhouse, several women were chatting so cheerfully with Suzanne that she almost forgot what was going to happen inside the brick building. Almost but not quite.

Chapter Two

A Painful Initiation

Suzanne and Michael were ushered into a large room. It was lavishly furnished in an expensive manner and with great attention to the tiniest detail. The room seemed to be leftover from another period. It should have looked tacky but instead, it had grace and charm. The walls had dark mahogany wainscoting, with plush red and gold velvet flocked wallpaper. There was deep, plush, chocolate carpet on most of the floor, with a large expanse of gleaming hardwood. Three large crystal chandeliers and crystal and brass wall sconces lined the walls of the room. At one end of the long room there was a raised platform, and at the other was a gleaming mahogany bar with brass trim. The bar was complete with bartender, a slender young man with a mustache who was wearing a white shirt and red suspenders with red garters on his shirtsleeves.

Suzanne later learned that the door beside the platform led to a professional, modern kitchen capable of serving large formal banquets, and a laundry room complete with linen closet. There were about two dozen soft, padded and comfortable chairs with deep velvet cushions.

The chairs were a far step up from the ones Suzanne usually found at clubs or symposiums. These chairs were definitely not the usual tacky, metal folding chairs she was used to finding at lectures, club functions or even the stackable chairs favored by some of the better hotels in their banquet rooms.

Seeing her appraisal of the chairs, Jerry, the chauffeur, came over to stand beside her. "We like to have very comfortable chairs. All our surroundings are very nice, of course, but we need the comfortable chairs because our bottoms are usually a little, umm, tender before the evening's over." He grinned at her discomfiture as he walked away.

On the platform at the front of the room there was a microphone and three plush armchairs for the host, James, and for Michael and Suzanne. Off to one side there was what could only be described as a whipping bench. Suzanne shuttered as she looked at it, chills running down her spine. The bench was about four feet long and almost waist high. It was thickly padded with plush, red velvet and furnished with several velvet straps.

A tall, gleaming brass bucket next to the bench held several assorted canes. The canes did not look very harsh. They were just lengths of slender bamboo, of varying thickness, from very thin to as broad as her thumb. Some had a crooked handle and some were just straight. How Victorian, Suzanne thought with another shiver, remembering the books she'd read at James' suggestion.

There were two more padded benches in the room; they were both lower and narrower than the bench on the dais. Those two benches were on the main floor, between the platform and the first row of the chairs facing it.

Off to one side of the dais there was a Victorian love seat. All three benches and the love seat were padded and upholstered in the same red velvet. Along one side of the room there was a hallway with several doors that, according to Michael, led to small, private bedrooms. A staircase led to still more bedrooms upstairs, and downstairs to a play dungeon and a storage area.

"Boy! I can hardly wait to drag you into one of those bedrooms and fuck you with your bottom red and on fire!" Michael was wildly enthusiastic. "I can just imagine your pain as I pound your burning ass into the mattress."

At Jerry's suggestion, Suzanne and Michael were seated in the special place of prominence on the raised platform, facing the group of about thirty club members. Just then James, the host for the evening, came in and introduced himself.

"Hello, I'm James. You must be Suzanne." He held out his hand and when she reached out her hand, he didn't shake hands with her but instead held her hand in a long warm grasp. "I'm

19

sorry to be so late, it's really inexcusable I know, but I got tied up at work." He winked, "Unfortunately that wasn't literally, it was only a metaphor."

Suzanne was pleased that the man she had spoken to on the phone turned out to be as warm in person. He was also a very good looking man about thirty years old, with short, curly blond hair. He was tall, with a slender yet athletic build and the most amazingly soft, friendly blue eyes.

Giving Suzanne a cheerful smile, he revealed a dimple in his left cheek before stepping up to the microphone. He started the meeting with an announcement that besides bringing such a lovely, prospective member for the club – he turned and gave Suzanne a warm look – Michael had been kind enough to volunteer to whip some of the regular members. He would do it now, before Suzanne's initiation.

Several club members, mainly women, lined up next to one of the padded benches. There was a tall brass bucket, like the one on the platform, filled with canes. A small, ornate table off to one side held several paddles and straps.

The large middle-aged woman at the front of the line laid herself over the bench, and the ones in line behind her pinned up her long, peach silk dress. She wore no underwear. Michael reached into the bucket, pulled out a long, thin cane and gave her a sound whipping. It turned her full, firm butt bright red. He kept up the whipping until she pulled up and said, "ENOUGH!"

Michael hesitated visibly before he gave the next person in line, which happened to be a slender young man, the same treatment. Michael continued, topping the members. Some members asked Michael to use a strap or a paddle instead of a cane, and he did as he was asked. It went on until there were no more club members waiting in line. There was a pause for a round of drinks and some socializing.

James made another announcement and it was one that startled Suzanne, but it would not be her only surprise at the meeting. She was to be the one to administer the next round of whippings. Hearing this announcement Michael was clearly shocked. His eyes widened and he opened his mouth to speak before he caught himself.

"Don't let the fact that they are going to whip you next prevent you from laying it on really hard, that would only make them mad!" James leaned over and whispered in her ear.

"But I've never done this before." Suzanne was almost pleading, "What if I hurt someone?"

"Then that someone will just thank you and move away." James grinned. "Unlike you, they've all been here before. They expect it to hurt. They even want it to hurt, just remember to stop when they ask you to."

Suzanne had her hands full. Many more members lined up to be whipped by her than lined up for Michael. The first person in line was her new friend, Jerry, the limo driver. She took a long, deep breath, looked at the pale, fleshy buttocks in front of her, raised the paddle he'd requested, and began to paddle him.

She felt strange as she slashed the paddles, whips and straps down on the various bare bottoms that were paraded in front of her. There was such a sense of unreality that she hardly noticed the individuals as real people, only seeing their behinds. It was almost as though they were only disembodied butts.

For the first few spankings James had to urge her on, pushing her to greater severity. He pushed her to use the paddle more and more harshly. She had never done anything like it before, but soon a sort of blood lust took over and she became almost ruthless. When she was done, her arm was sore and there was another small break for more refreshments. James offered to bring cocktails for Suzanne and Michael.

"I'll have a scotch and water," Michael said, "but bring Suzanne straight soda water. We wouldn't want the liquor to dull her fear or her pain!" He explained with a mean-spirited laugh.

James gave Michael a wicked smile before he went to the bar. He brought Michael a very mild scotch and soda, but brought Suzanne a very strong gin and tonic! As he handed the icy glass to Suzanne their hands met for a timeless moment and she looked up into his warm eyes, shocked. Even with the drink she began to get very nervous and frightened, close to panic. She knew her own whipping was to be the next item on the agenda.

"Damn weak drink!" Michael complained. "I didn't expect to get watered drinks at a ritzy club like this!"

All too soon, at least in Suzanne's mind, James came up to her. With a friendly smile and a courtly bow he took both her hands and helped her stand up. Her nerves were stretched so tight that her legs were threatening to buckle, as if they would not be able to support her without James holding her hands. She finally understood why those girls were so compliant; the fear and arousal was hypnotic. She stared into James' warm and friendly eyes.

She was so scared, yet so mesmerized, that she hardly noticed Michael walking around behind her, and barely felt him unzipping her dress. He pushed the dress off her arms so that it slid down her sensuous body and fell in a blue puddle at her feet. Suzanne's awareness returned as she felt the cool air on her skin, but James still held her hands. She forced herself to keep staring into his eyes as Michael unsnapped her silky brassiere, then slid her lacy panties down her legs.

Suzanne was in such an emotional fugue that she hardly even noticed she was standing in front of a crowd naked except for her garter belt and stockings. She felt none of the embarrassment she had expected to feel. Indeed, she felt very little of the fear she had expected to feel. All she felt was the cool air on her skin and the reassurance coming to her from the warmth of James' smile. She hardly saw the group of club members around her. All she really saw was James' warm eyes looking into hers.

James led her firmly over to the special bench, the one with the straps for her ankles, waist and wrists. Suzanne moved woodenly, as if she were in a daze. James still held her hands while Michael strapped her feet to the bench legs.

James said softly but with firm command, "Bend over, Suzanne."

He kissed her hands and pulled her gently but firmly forward.

Michael quickly fastened the straps at her waist, and then she realized that she couldn't move. It was happening! Fear, excitement and arousal raced through her blood. James fastened the straps to her wrists. He positioned her so that her head was on a soft padded pillow.

He gave her a quick light kiss on her neck and with a wink said, "Don't worry, my dear, it won't be so bad." He smiled down at her. "Besides you have no choice now, you can hardly squirm, let alone move. Now all you can do is let it happen. Think of it as a challenge. See if you can endure this without using the code words, but please remember not to hesitate to use them if you need to."

It was true, she realized, she was completely immobilized. The only uncomfortable part of her restraint was the way she was laying. Her breasts were too large and full for her to be very comfortable on her stomach. She knew she could scream all she wanted but it would not bring her any mercy or any help. Luckily it would not bring her any extra punishment either; this was no Victorian novel, and she could end things at her will. The only things that could stop the caning would be for her to use the code word, or start to bleed or a signal from James. Other than that, every member present would cane her. She tried to breathe deeply, tried to will herself to relax. Of course she failed miserably; any degree of relaxation was impossible.

"I think you need a warm up," James said softly.

He began to spank her with his hands, beginning with light smacks and building ever so slowly in speed and intensity. Soon her whole bottom began to feel warm and tingly. James stopped spanking her.

He picked up the cane, held it for a long moment against her butt, and then tapped her with it several times before he raised his arm and the dreadful whipping began.

He slashed her smooth, softly rounded ass. Suzanne gasped out loud as the cane landed. The pain intensified even as she heard the cane whistle in the air for the second cut. By the third cut her gasps became high-pitched yelps. Cut after cut, the pain grew into agony and a trace of something else. Although she didn't realize it, James wasn't really being very severe. After about a dozen slashing strokes James gave the rod to the next person in line.

He was a slim, young man who gave her six or seven strokes and used the cane faster and just a little harder than James did. At each swish of the cane Suzanne flinched visibly, and as every blow landed she screamed out loud but somehow she avoided using the code word. She struggled uselessly against the straps binding her. There was now definitely something there, another feeling other than pain. It was almost a sexual excitement.

The young man handed the cane off to the next person in line who happened to be the chauffeur, Jerry. Again, he preferred a paddle so he put the cane down and spent a few moments selecting a paddle. It gave her a short respite. Jerry paddled her about a dozen strokes smartly but almost playfully, not really very harshly. Suzanne almost enjoyed them. He put down the paddle and moved off.

After five people had given her spankings, she began to feel tired and numb. James was watching her carefully; abruptly he gave a silent signal and immediately the rest of the people waiting in line pulled back and the spanking was stopped.

There was a short pause, then just as she began to relax, it was Michael's turn. Michael gave her four final and hard, devastating blows with a large, wooden paddle. The surface of the paddle was about 10" x 4", it was about an inch thick and there was a six-inch handle. Each blow made a loud, sharp crack as it landed. Few people failed to notice that the crack of the paddle as it landed on Suzanne's round, firm ass was almost drowned out by her loud, high-pitched yells.

The paddle did indeed make a lot of noise as it landed on her bare bottom but it was made of light wood, and didn't hurt as much as it sounded like it would. The paddle didn't draw any blood but it stung and made her already sore buttocks throb and hurt terribly.

As Michael began to swing the paddle a fifth time, James

caught his hand in a firm grip and took away the paddle. "That's enough!"

The ordeal was finally over.

James unfastened her and led her over to the love seat. He told her to lie on her stomach while he gently rubbed a soothing balm all over her backside. Then he put a cold, damp cloth on her bottom, which was red and blotchy. After he finished tending to her he gave her a glass of cold champagne.

"I don't know whether to drink this or to pour it on my ass," she quipped weakly.

"Drink it." James smiled. "It really does work much more effectively taken internally. By the way, your butt has a lot of very interesting colors to it. It looks very pretty."

"Gee, thanks a lot." Suzanne sipped her champagne.

"I want to fuck her now!" Michael said, coming over to stand beside James, "While she's still really sore! Get in the room, Suzanne." He pointed to one of the bedrooms.

"I'm sorry, Michael," James interjected sternly, "but you'll have to wait. The initiation isn't over yet." There was a trace of hidden delight as he told Michael, "The best is yet to come. Let's sit down while Suzanne recovers for a moment."

"You mean she's got more coming to her?" Michael was excited, "Great! I can hardly wait."

"I'm sure you'll enjoy the remainder of the evening," James told the older man, smiling coolly. "In fact, I can guarantee it."

Chapter Three

A Surprise Initiation

Before the meeting proceeded any further there was another round of drinks and socializing. Some of the club members walked over to talk to Suzanne and see how she was doing. They seemed so gentle and concerned for her that Suzanne was surprised and touched. When the drinks were served, once again Michael got an extremely weak cocktail.

Suzanne, who was still naked for some reason, was not embarrassed a bit by her nudity. She was about to get up from the love seat to go and get herself a drink, but James offered to wait on her. He brought her some more cold champagne.

After the refreshments and a short pause, James made another announcement, the one that was a complete surprise for Michael. Surprise is far too weak a word for it; this came as a total shock, and not a pleasant one. Not pleasant at all.

"Well Michael, it's your turn to undress and assume the position over the whipping bench," James ordered sternly, in a voice that brooked no refusal, "NOW!"

James had not liked this man from the moment he'd first spoken to him. To him Michael was a not a spanko, he was an abusive jerk. James had long since decided to teach the older man a lesson. The club rules were that all spankings were voluntary but James decided not to mention that to Michael. What he was doing was against the club rules but a man had to do what a man had to do.

Michael looked around the room with fear in his eyes and he immediately saw two things: First, he really had no choice but to comply. There were too many strong men in the room and they were all more than willing to help strap him down forcibly, and second, Suzanne wasn't at all surprised. She had known

26

somehow what was in store for him and she had not even warned him.

Michael sent her a look filled with so much anger and hatred that it made her realize she was in very real danger from him. She would have to find a way to avoid being alone with Michael. That may be hard to do, she thought, since he had a key to her house. Suddenly she was very afraid.

Along with her fear, a fury of her own began to build up within her. She was angry at Michael's idea that it was great fun for her to be publicly whipped but apparently not as much fun to be whipped himself. WIMP! She began to long for the feel of the paddle in her hands, but she was careful to keep her feelings hidden.

"James, I want to be the one to strap Michael down," she volunteered softly, getting to her feet very slowly.

Her voice was very sweet and gentle, just as gentle as she was when she fastened the straps so very tightly to Michael's ankles, wrists and hands.

"Ouch! Damn it woman! That hurts!" Michael protested, "You stupid cow, you've fastened the straps much too tight. Loosen them, now!"

"Calling me a stupid cow is a very strange way to get me to loosen them, Michael," she said very coldly. "So I'll have to decline."

"You stupid bitch!" Michael yelled, the veins in his neck standing out, "I'll get you for this!"

Ignoring the outburst, James gave Michael the first dozen strokes with the cane and they were much harder cuts than the ones he had given Suzanne. They were very severe cuts indeed. Next in line were all the members who had not been able to cane Suzanne before James decided her whipping had to be stopped. These members took turns using the cane to whip Michael's ass. They all whipped Michael severely. He fought the straps and screamed much louder than Suzanne had! He shouted everything except the code word!

James smiled to himself; it was unfortunate for Michael that no one bothered to tell him the code word. It was also unfortunate for Michael that he had such tough skin. Before Michael finally started to bleed all the members, even some who had whipped Suzanne, had a chance to whip Michael too. And for some strange reason, they all wanted to whip Michael and whip him hard.

Finally, Suzanne's turn came to use the paddle on Michael and she was utterly without mercy. She never realized that she was given a different paddle to use; it looked the same but it was made of much heavier wood. This time James did not stop the beating at a measly four blows. He let Suzanne give Michael a full dozen harsh smacks!

The moment Suzanne finished using the paddle on Michael, the club was declared adjourned. Michael did not get any soothing balm put on his wounds or a cool cloth, or any cold and refreshing champagne. For that matter, he did not even get any time to recover!

Michael and Suzanne were escorted into the enclosed garage. They were a funny sight since they were both still naked except for Michael's shoes and socks, and Suzanne's stockings and garter belt, and of course the multitude of welts and bruises both of them wore on their buttocks and legs.

The club members walked along behind them and looked at the red blotches on both of their bottoms. They discussed the two prospective members quietly amongst themselves. When the group reached the limo, James made one additional announcement.

"I'm sorry to announce that you have been blackballed, Michael." James smiled, not looking sorry at all. He turned and smiled warmly at Suzanne, "However, you have been accepted, Suzanne. Welcome to the Paddle Club. We are honored to have you join us."

"She can't join without me!" Michael protested loudly, "and I wouldn't join this bunch of losers if you paid me."

"Then it's a good thing we don't want you," James said coldly.

"Suzanne, come with me," Michael barked. "Now!"

"Shut up Michael!" She snapped surprising him into silence, before turning to James. "I'm very honored that you have accepted me," Suzanne continued, although she was still not really sure if she wanted to participate in the club.

She would decide later, she thought; maybe even attend a regular party where she wasn't the victim of the day, just to see how it went.

Michael was torn in two; he wasn't sure whether he felt insulted or glad to be rejected. He really hadn't liked being whipped! All he ever wanted to get from attending the initiation was an excuse to whip and torment Suzanne. He sighed philosophically to himself; at least he would still be able to torment Suzanne. Imagine her ordering him around that way, telling him to shut up! And what about keeping his whipping a secret from him? He would get revenge, and he would get it on that bitch's bare backside.

The chauffeur, Jerry, opened the limo door and Suzanne got in. Her dress and Michael's rented tuxedo were folded into two neat piles, waiting on the back seat.

As Michael started to get in Suzanne said very sweetly, "I really think I'm going to like the club, now that the initiation is over." Mentally, she had her fingers crossed. "I do want to thank you for bringing me, Michael, but I have finally realized something. I don't love you anymore. In fact, I don't even like you anymore. Please find another way home."

"Suzanne!" Michael protested. "I brought you here!"

"And you'll leave me here," she replied calmly. "Contrary to your belief, I am not stupid. I will never let myself be alone with you again. You've changed since we met. You are now a cruel and hateful man, who wants revenge for doing to you what you wanted to do to me."

"Suzanne! No! I love you," Michael protested, knowing that she was right. "I would never want to hurt you. How could you even think such a thing?"

Suzanne ignored him and turned to face James. That's when she got the biggest shock of the night. When their eyes met it was stunning! It was as if there was an electric current flowing between her and James. Everything and everyone else faded out of her consciousness.

In a soft, shaky voice she said, "James, would you be so kind as to escort me home?"

She threw Michael's tuxedo unceremoniously out the car door. It landed on an oil spot.

Sounding equally stunned, James replied, "I'd be honored to escort you." He gave her a big, warm smile as he got into the limo beside her.

"I'll be back," Jerry said curtly, and before anyone could react, he picked up Michael's tuxedo and got into the limo.

Jerry started the limo and they drove away. The other members soon drifted off. Michael was left standing there waiting all alone. Until Jerry returned he was stranded and naked. Now, at last, he was no big shot. Not at all.

Sitting comfortably on the plush cushions, James looked at Suzanne. "I know it's too soon for me to say this, way too soon, because I realize that you are a lady in every sense of the word. I want you to know I would really like to make love with you, but maybe when we get to know each other a little better," he smiled gently, "if that's what you want."

She searched his smiling face, remembering how kind and reassuring he'd been all through the meeting, even when he was whipping her. She looked at him long and hard, silently, as she made her decision.

"I'm glad you think I'm a lady, James, I do try to be one," she said with a soft smile, "but I'm not so ladylike that I would deny us both something wonderful. I don't want to wait and get to know you better; that will come. I just want to make love to you, right here and now."

He looked a little bit surprised, and very glad. "I can hardly wait to get you home."

She looked around and found the button that slid the one way glass up between them and Jerry. "Why wait?" The question managed to sound both innocent and mischievous at the same time.

In front, Jerry was very much aware of exactly why the glass was up and he was secretly delighted. He turned some soft music on and hummed to himself, thinking of his own sweet wife at home. She had skipped the meeting, which was unusual for her because an old friend of hers was visiting from out of town. Jerry knew that most of the club members would be shocked if they knew what he planned to do to his wife and with his wife when he got home. He would make love to her in many ways long into the night. In spite of his age, Jerry was not old. Neither was his wife.

In the back seat, with a move that surprised James, Suzanne unzipped his pants and took him into her mouth. After several moments she took her mouth away from him.

"I want you inside me," she said looking up at him with her wet mouth.

She moved quickly and sat straddling his legs. With James guiding her, she lifted herself up and came down on his cock. James reached up to fondle her large breasts, while she moved up and down on him, driving him wild. It was fast and furious as they reached a frenzied orgasm together. In the afterglow, James took care of her, holding her on his lap and gently rubbing some lotion over her still tender bottom. The red was already fading to pink, except for a few dark blotches.

As they cuddled gently, she looked at him and said, "You were the only person at the meeting who didn't have a whipping tonight, from either of us. Don't you like to be the one on the receiving end?"

"It depends on my mood. Usually I'm a top but once in a while I love to be a bottom. Tonight was different, however, as the host, I was too busy. I wanted to make everything as good for you as possible, especially with that dumb jackass around. God! I'm so glad you dumped him!" He nibbled her ear.

"I should hope so, after the sex we just had!" She kissed him hungrily, and quipped, "I just hope I didn't blow my image as a lady when I blew you."

"You're always a lady," James said sincerely, his hands firmly but not cruelly grasping her behind.

"Even with your cock in my mouth?" she asked with a grin and wink.

"Especially with my cock in your mouth." He kissed her before asking the question that had plagued him all night. "Suzanne, why were you with that jerk in the first place? How could you have loved him?"

Suzanne smiled ruefully as she explained, "I know I should have dumped Michael long ago, but I could never force myself to believe he wouldn't change back to the man he used to be. Anyway, I would never have met you if I had dumped him," she gave him a long, slow, passionate kiss, "and I have a strong feeling that you're worth about a hundred times what he's worth, certainly worth any pain he caused me."

The romantic moment was interrupted by the intercom. "I don't mean to intrude," they heard Jerry's amused voice over the speaker, "but I want to be sure before I go any further. Do you want me to take you to Suzanne's home or to yours, James?"

"Would you come home with me, Suzanne?" James asked in a surprisingly shy voice.

"Yes, love. I'd love to go home with you," Suzanne answered.

James kissed her gently, and then spoke to Jerry, "We'll go to my place."

"Good idea, sir. I'm glad you thought of it," Jerry laughed.

"Thanks Jerry," James said softly.

After a very short time, the limo pulled to a stop in front of James' house. Jerry was wise enough not to get out and open the limo door. Instead, he waited while the couple rearranged their clothes and got out themselves.

Suzanne leaned in through the limo window and spoke to Jerry, "It was very nice meeting you, Jerry. Have a nice night."

He gave her a kiss on the cheek and sighed dramatically. "Why does he get all the pretty girls?"

"I don't know," Suzanne whispered in Jerry's ear, "but I'm going to be the last pretty girl he gets if I have anything so say about it."

She looked James over lewdly before she turned back to Jerry and winked at him, "You're certainly much better looking." Behind her, James made an exaggerated choking sound. "Maybe it's because you're already married."

"I'll tell the missus you said that. After thirty-eight years, I think she takes me for granted." Jerry gave Suzanne a big smile and started the car ready to drive away, after saying, "I'll try to remind her of what a good catch I am tonight when I get home."

"I'll bet she's well aware of what a catch you are," Suzanne told him. "She's kept you for thirty-eight years."

"What do you mean he's better looking?" James teased, as the limo disappeared. He held his front door open for her. "If you weren't already so sore, you'd pay for that remark."

"I'll start quaking in my boots." She walked past him into the house, turned to face him and shot him a mischievous grin. "Later."

"I still have one question, what did you whisper in Jerry's ear?" James asked curiously.

"You'll never know." She smiled, with a grin so filled with secret pleasure that James forgot the question in his desire to get her into his bed.

Chapter Four

A New Lover

James had a beautiful, comfortable house on a large lot at the edge of town. It was fairly new, custom built and very modern. When Suzanne got inside she looked around, studying her surroundings. He had a large living room that was clean and neat, with off-white walls and comfortable, leather furniture all covered in earth tones, with lots of throw pillows in shades of blue, rose and turquoise. Along one wall he had a large, impressive looking entertainment center. It was made of black lacquered wood and held a stereo, CD player, flat screen television and VCR. He had an extensive collection of CD's and videotapes. The CD's ranged from rock to jazz and even some classical.

She looked at the videos; they seemed to contain all the latest hit movies along with several children's classics. After asking James' permission, she opened a small cabinet that could be locked if necessary, which contained more videos. There were spanking videos and a few others that seemed much more adult.

"James, do the club members know you have these tapes?" she asked him innocently.

"The spanky ones?" James answered, puzzled, "I don't really know. Why?"

"Not those ones, silly, all the kiddie cartoons." She winked at him. "They seem a little out of character."

"Not for a man with two nieces and three nephews living in town, they're not," he told her.

Another wall was filled with an extensive and varied collection of books. Suzanne walked over and looked at the covers. She saw everything from political commentary to a lurid crime novel, in both paperback and hardcover.

Off to one side, Suzanne could see into a gleaming, white modern kitchen. On the other side was a hallway. James walked up, stood behind Suzanne, and slid his arms around her waist.

"Can I get you something?" he whispered in her ear, sending shivers down her spine. "Some wine? Coffee? A late night snack?"

She turned to face him and said boldly, "Right now, a bed would come in real, real handy."

James scooped her up in his arms, laughing and carried her into the bedroom. "Will this one do?" he said, dropping her unceremoniously on the king-size bed, ignoring her still tender bottom.

She laughed and reached up for him, "Only if you're in it with me."

He bent down to kiss her, then straightened up and began to remove his clothes. Taking his cue, she rolled off the bed and turned her back to him, allowing him to unzip her formal, and very wrinkled blue satin dress.

She stood before him in her lacy black bra and garter belt, her waist long hair falling over her left shoulder, like a silky black curtain covering her breast. Watching in silent approval as he undressed, she enjoyed her first look at his slim but athletic body, and his large cock. She thought it was strange, she had tasted that cock, and felt it inside her, and yet had never really seen it. It was long, thick, erect and beautiful.

He stepped behind her and unfastened her bra, gently cupping her large breasts from behind and teasing the nipples with his fingers. He unsnapped her garter belt without unfastening her hose, and peeled her stockings and garter belt off all in one piece.

He backed her up against the bed, and together they pulled down the burgundy velvet comforter. Lifting her onto the bed, this time he followed her down. He moved over her, supporting his weight on his arms and began to kiss her, starting at her mouth and moving ever so slowly down to her neck. His kisses trailed down her body, slathering one breast then the other with his moist, warm tongue. She shivered with the pleasure he gave her.

His mouth continued its path down her body. He held her hands in his, preventing her from doing anything to him, and using only his mouth, he explored her luscious body. He stopped for a moment to explore her navel before his mouth went still lower. Slowly, ever so slowly, his mouth found the silky tangle of curls at the apex of her thighs. He released one of her hands and slid his arm under her leg, raising it up on his shoulders. He grasped that hand again and repeated the procedure with the other leg. Raising his head and smiling tenderly at her, he finally, slowly lowered his mouth to her tender succulent cunt. She was writhing with pleasure.

He played with her, sucking, licking, and even nipping at her tender flesh until she came with an orgasm that left her breathless. Releasing her hands, he climbed up her body until he reached her mouth, kissing her passionately.

"This is how we taste together," he murmured.

"That was incredible," she said, smiling contentedly, "but I still want to feel your cock inside me again."

"I aim to please." He kissed her and slid into the warmth of her, making love to her gently for a short time, until they both built up to a crashing climax.

As they cuddled together in the tangled sheets afterwards James said, "I'm hungry. Let's go raid the refrigerator."

"I'm sleepy," Suzanne moaned.

"But I'll bet you're hungry, too. I know I am. I'll also bet," James grinned at her, "that you didn't eat any dinner tonight, um, last night. I mean before the party."

"How did you guess?" She nibbled his neck.

He got out of bed and handed her a terry cloth knee-length white robe. Reaching into the closet, he pulled on a royal blue one. "Because I was too scared to eat before my initiation, and I knew more about what I was getting into than you did."

She pulled on the robe and taking his hand, followed him downstairs. He pulled some roast beef out of the refrigerator and they had thick roast beef sandwiches, with milk. Then they each had some homemade apple pie.

"Did you make this?" Suzanne asked surprised, she knew it wasn't a frozen pie.

"I wish I could say I did, but I had dinner with my folks the night before last and Mom sent it home with me, the roast beef, too." James grinned at her. "She's always afraid I'm not eating right."

"My mother's the same way." Suzanne smiled, "I wonder when they're going to think of us as grown-ups?"

"I hope never, if it keeps her baking like this." James laughed before taking a big bite of the pie.

The next morning they made love again before they got out of bed. Then they made love, wildly but carefully, in the shower. James inspected her bruises, which weren't very bad after all. He loaned her a pair of red jogging shorts and a white T-shirt. He pulled out a similar pair of shorts for himself, and a tank top. They both dressed and went downstairs to make breakfast.

Over a simple breakfast of toast, orange juice and scrambled eggs, they talked. They started by discussing the club. James cleared something up that had been bothering her. He told her that the club did not discriminate, but applications from Asians and Blacks were rare. In fact, he told her there was only one Black couple in the club but they had not been able to attend the initiation. The conversation turned to her. She told James about her one worry leftover from the previous night. Michael still had a key to her house.

"We can solve that after we finish having our breakfast," James said.

He took her home, stopping at a hardware store on the way. As soon as they arrived home, she knew there had been reason for her concern; Michael's car was gone and two of the tires on her own car were slashed. Inside the house there was no damage but she could tell Michael had been there, as most of his clothes were gone from her closet. She quickly called the police.

James had her get out her tools and with her help, installed new locks and put an alarm on her door. By the time the police arrived, she had packed up the last of Michael's things that she could still find at her place and put them in a box in her garage. She reported the slashed tires, and told the police why she suspected Michael. After they left, she packed some clothes and put on her floral print one-piece bathing suit, under a full skirt.

They stopped at her landlord's home on their way back to James' house. They gave the landlord one of the new keys and told him about the alarm. Suzanne explained that she had broken up with Michael, told him about her tires, and asked him not to let Michael have a copy of the new key. She introduced James to him.

Her landlord, a burly ex-navy man with tattoos on his forearms, surprised her by hugging her lightly and saying, "I'm glad you broke up with that creep. Don't worry, Honey, I'll see that he doesn't bother you anymore." Then he looked James over. "You treat her right now, you hear?"

"I sure will," James smiled at the man, "and give me a call if the creep gives Suzanne or even you any trouble."

"I can take care of him." The tough, older landlord smiled tightly as he shook hands with James. "Don't you worry."

"He looks like he could take care of a dozen Michaels," James told Suzanne, "I have a feeling I'd better treat you real nice."

"I have a feeling you would anyway." Suzanne kissed him, grinning.

Finally, they went back to James' house. James put on navy swimming trunks and they went for a swim in his pool. Afterwards they laid out, lounging on towels on the redwood deck, soaking in the hot sun and talking.

"We started this relationship a little bit backwards," James said. "We had sex before we really got to know each other. I usually don't do that. That's something I want you to understand, I play my spanky games, but I don't actually have sex with someone or bring her here unless I really care for her." James reached out to gently stroke her silky hair.

"I've never jumped into bed with anyone I just met either," Suzanne replied. "Not before last night. I may try to hang on to

38

a relationship for far too long, but I've never started one so quickly. I must admit though it feels right, wonderful and completely natural being here with you."

"It feels right for me, too. And amazing." James kissed her. The kiss built up quickly. "Let's go inside, my love."

When they got inside, James took her upstairs to his bedroom. He had a startling request for Suzanne. He opened his closet and took out a leather western belt, hand-tooled and heavy. He stood next to the bed and asked her to use his belt to give him a good hard whipping.

"Why do you want a whipping now?" she asked curiously, surprised.

"I can give you three reasons: First, I didn't get a whipping last night at the party."

"Poor, deprived baby," Suzanne said with false sympathy.

"Depraved, more likely," his mouth twisted ruefully, "but the second reason is more important. I want to make sure you really understand that our relationship won't be just one sided. You won't always be the bottom. Our love life won't just consist of my whipping or abusing you. In fact, except for the club we probably won't play our little spanky games all that often, and we'll do it only when we both feel like it," James paused. "Your poor ex-boyfriend made a mistake when he tried to join our club. As I tried to explain on the phone, many S & M clubs are strictly for dominates and submissives. Our club isn't quite that way. We're made up of people who enjoy spankings and role playing, and most of them enjoy it from either side. Most of our members do have a role they favor; but very few members go home from a party without doing both, getting and giving discipline."

"Where was I?" James continued, "I remember, third, a whipping always gives me a hard-on, although with you around, getting a hard-on doesn't seem like it's going to be much of a problem."

She directed him to lay face down on the bed. He did. She began to whip him with his belt, but not very hard. He grabbed her hand and stopped her.

"Come on, Love, get tough, you won't hurt me," he said, kissing her. "Remember, I've been on the receiving end many times and I enjoy it."

She began to whip him again, with a lot more vigor this time. Red welts appeared on his lean, tan buttocks. She kept whipping him until he asked her to stop. He rolled over revealing an enormous erection. She stepped out of her bathing suit. He reached up and without speaking a word, and pulled her down on top of him. From that night on they were a couple, in every sense of the word.

Chapter Five

A Life Together Begins

After Suzanne and James had been lovers for a few weeks, she gave up her small apartment and moved into his house with him. They got along famously, with similar views and interests in many ways, but with enough differences to make life interesting. For one thing, Suzanne was a city girl down to her toes, and James liked camping. She liked animals and rode horses, and James had never had a pet of any kind. She loved sports cars. He rode a motorcycle sometimes. She was tougher on crime than James was, and they often got into debates on political issues.

Soon after they began living together they invited a couple from the Paddle Club over for dinner. The couple, Sherry and Clayton, was among their best friends in the club. They sat around the table discussing the club while eating the roast chicken and rice stuffing that Suzanne had prepared. It seemed that in addition to the regular parties, the club had planned some upcoming special club events. James and Suzanne were in charge of the next special event, something they called a Maze, and much to Sherry's frustration, they were both being very close-mouthed about it.

"You'll just have to wait and go through it," Suzanne told her sternly, ending the discussion. "That's what you get for missing the meeting when we called for volunteers to plan it."

"I was sick!" Sherry pouted. "I had a fever, nausea, vomiting. All that stuff."

"So what? That's no excuse." James winked, as he sided with Suzanne. "I hope Clay punished you for missing the meeting."

"Sorry James, I never spank a woman who's been vomiting," Clay grinned, "I wouldn't want to risk ruining one of my suits."

After dinner everyone played a board game upon which James had made a few alterations. They were testing it out because he was hoping it would be something to use at the club. The club members were a playful bunch, even silly sometimes, and new ideas were always welcome.

The game was basically a standard board game but they altered the rules and renamed most of the spaces. They renamed it **Rewards and Punishments.**

The game consisted of a rectangular board with small squares along all four sides. The squares had different events on them. There were several squares that made anyone landing on them draw a card from one of two piles. One pile was for *Rewards* and the other was for *Punishments.*

The rules were as follows: Each player had to move their pieces around the board according to the roll of a die, from start to end. Depending on how long the players wanted the game to last, they could use from 1 to 4 pieces each.

Each player could have only one active piece on the board at a time, except when that piece was stranded on one of the last six squares from the end. For a piece to reach the end, the exact number needed to land on the END square must be rolled, or else a player must wait in place for another roll. It was at that time the player could start another piece, if that player had any pieces left to play.

If a player lands on a square that is occupied by another player, he sends that player back to the start. If a player lands on a starred square, he could send any player back to the start or he could change places with any other piece on the board.

If a player lands on a "P" or "R" he has to take a punishment card or a reward card. The punishments were of two kinds: game punishments, such as lose a turn, or go back to start; and physical punishments, such as lose an article of clothing, give another player a foot massage or accept a spanking from the player next to you.

The player would roll a pair of dice to see how many blows he was to receive. There was even a die, which was optional, to be used when the players wanted to use implements for the punishments. On its six sides the die had: Hand, paddle, crop, belt, hairbrush, and cane.

The rewards consisted of: game rewards, such as free spins and safety markers to prevent being sent back; and physical rewards such as getting a kiss, a back rub or even having one of the other players as a temporary slave.

Sherry, a pretty redhead with wavy shoulder length hair and amber eyes, got off to a good start with a four but she was sent back by James. Then Clayton rolled a five and Suzanne rolled a three.

On her second turn, Sherry rolled a five and sent Clayton back. A frown formed on Clay's handsome face as he was always a serious game player. Concentrating hard, he tightened his green eyes until they were almost slits. James rolled a four and Suzanne had another three, landing her on a starred square.

As the game progressed, James, Clayton and Sherry kept sending each other back. Suzanne kept to the route, but she landed on three punishments. The first punishment was a harsh spanking. She rolled the dice and got an eleven. She rolled the other die and got the paddle. Suzanne dropped her jeans and bent over, her hands holding the sides of the table. Clayton, sitting next to her, did the honors. Clayton was a perfectionist; he always had a stern, no-nonsense attitude whenever he was punishing anyone. He pushed up the sleeves on his sweater, revealing his muscular arm, and paddled her harshly with hard, slow blows. Each blow was given severely, spaced out just enough to let the pain build up before the next swing of the paddle, and each swat made a loud smack as it landed on Suzanne's bare butt. Halfway through, Suzanne began to gasp at each blow.

"Thanks a lot!" she told him with a rueful grin, pulling up her jeans and sitting down, but very gingerly. Her butt was throbbing!

Her second punishment was to lose a turn. Her third was to go back to the start. Her luck changed, however, when she finally landed on a reward square and pulled a card that had her going back to where she was previously. Then she got one more punishment. She lost her shirt. Literally. Unfortunately she wasn't wearing a bra.

Meanwhile the other players continued around the outside edge. Finally, James landed on a punishment square. He drew a spanking. He rolled a seven, and on the other die, a whip. Sherry whipped him, having him drop his pants and bend over the end of the sofa. She slashed the whip onto his bare buttocks slowly and used severe force, without any warm-up. James took his punishment in stoic silence but when Sherry finished with him he had red slash marks on his ass, suspiciously wet looking eyes and a huge hard-on.

Suzanne was ahead, but she was stalled with the first of her game pieces. Since she was on one of the last six squares, she started her second piece.

Sherry landed on a punishment square and drew her card; grinning she showed it to the others. She was to be tied up and teased by the other players.

From her expression, she made it clear that she didn't consider this a punishment. She soon found out that she was wrong; in mere minutes her rivals had her squirming in unfulfilled ecstasy. She was so highly aroused that she squirmed uncomfortably for the next half-hour.

The game continued for quite a while, with everyone having a good time; they all received their fair share of punishments and rewards.

By the time the game ended, all the players were naked and had bright red, stinging butts. James had his hands handcuffed behind his back. His erection had gone down at last, but it had taken a long time, and he had been uncomfortable for much of that time, especially since Suzanne had been assigned to reward him with a massage. She also had to roll the dice and move for him, but he received the punishments or the rewards. Sherry was the winner. The two couples got dressed and had coffee and spice cake for dessert, as they discussed the game.

That night, when Suzanne and James went up to bed they made

hot, passionate love. James asked her to roll onto her stomach, while he knelt on the bed between her legs. He played with her firm ass, squeezing it and pulling the sides apart. Leaning forward, he even kissed and gently nipped it. He slapped her butt a few times, not very hard, just hard enough to warm it up and put his hands on her hips, pulling her up onto her hands and knees.

In one smooth motion he slid his cock into her vagina. He began to move within her, in a slow, gentle motion. Gradually he slid in and out of the moist velvet sheath. Slowly, ever so slowly, he built up the speed. Suzanne tossed her head, her long, silky black hair brushing James' face. James grabbed the end of her hair with one hand, holding it just tight enough against her neck to cause Suzanne to raise her head. Finally, he brought her to a crashing, wonderful climax, before letting himself go with a long, loud moaning yell.

She rolled over, breathing heavily. He gently took her into his arms. She cuddled up against him and ran a long fingernail around on his chest, teasing his nipples and playing with his chest hair. Before long her gentle touch had the desired effect.

"Hey, little girl. If you keep that up we won't get any sleep," James growled lazily in her ear, holding her close.

"Hey, big man. If you keep that up," she reached down and gently fondled his large erection, "we won't want any sleep."

Chapter Six

What Santa Gives Good Girls

At regular Paddle Club parties, that is parties when there was no initiation being held, the members didn't usually dress formally. They saved that for the club's initiations. At the other parties, they were usually dressed in casual clothes, sometimes with costumes at Halloween. A few of the ladies wore corsets, with lacy garters and stockings. Almost all the ladies wore silky, lacy panties.

A few of the members more into BDSM would wear black leather or latex outfits decorated with silver studs, every now and then. Suzanne still thought the outfits were tacky. For herself, she preferred to dress in casual and comfortable street clothes. Of course on her, almost anything she wore looked elegant.

At one party, between Thanksgiving and Christmas, Suzanne was wearing a full red skirt and a red, green and white sweater. She wandered away from James when she spotted Jerry across the room. Jerry had become one of her favorite members and one of her best friends. On this occasion, in honor of the holidays, he had come to the party dressed as Santa Claus. It was surprising how little effort it took for Jerry to make a fantastic Santa. He already had the roly-poly shape, he was the right age and he had a very merry grin, with rosy cheeks and twinkling eyes. All he needed was the suit and a beard. He was seated on one of the large overstuffed chairs near the dais.

Suzanne went over to greet him. "Hi, Santa." She kissed his cheek.

"Ho! Ho! Ho!" Jerry said merrily. "Come up and sit on my lap little girl."

When Suzanne sat herself on his lap Jerry said, "Have you been a good little girl?"

"Well . . ." Suzanne looked at him with innocence in her big blue eyes, "I try to be good, Santa, sort of."

"What do you mean, sort of?" Jerry asked her sternly, "Are you a bad girl sometimes?"

"Well, sometimes, maybe," Suzanne said softly, with an air of meekness, "I might do something bad once in a while."

"Have you at least been punished for all the wrong things you've done?" Santa Jerry asked. "Or has James been neglecting you?"

Suzanne replied ingenuously, "Well, I don't always tell James when I've been bad." She leaned forward and whispered in Jerry's ear, "And sometimes, he even makes me do bad things, Santa, I can't lie to you."

"Well, I guess I can bring you a little gift, just for being so honest. What do you want, girl?" he asked her.

"I want a hot, red bottom, Santa, please," she replied, smiling.

"Santa can do that, little girl. I'll give you your present right now if you lay face down across my lap." His green eyes twinkled.

Suzanne got into the required position, draped across his lap with her long, black hair brushing the floor. She felt him raise her full, red skirt up onto her back, and gently lower the silky red underwear down her legs. Jerry rubbed her buttocks gently, then he began to spank her with firm, loud, cracking slaps.

He took his time warming her up. He turned one side of her butt red and hot, and then changed his attention to the other side. When he had spanked both cheeks until they were red and hot, without causing any real pain, he started over.

This time, he spanked her harder, again first on one side and then on the other. The spanking went on for a long time, gradually getting harsher and harsher. Suzanne squirmed and gasped occasionally but she kept silent for over seventy blows, until her butt was red and on fire.

Finally, she said, "Thank you, Santa, that's enough."

Jerry pulled her underwear the rest of the way off and lowered her skirt. He handed her the lacy panties and kissed her on the cheek. When he looked up, there was a line of people waiting their turn on Santa's lap.

One of the club members came over to talk to Suzanne. His name was Alan, a tall lanky blond man with an amiable manner.

"Hey Alan, what's new?" Suzanne kissed him on the cheek.

"I've met a terrific girl," Alan said blushing. "We've been dating for about a month now. She's sweet, and smart and very beautiful."

"Are you going to bring her here so we can meet her?" Suzanne asked, with a grin. "I want to tell her all your dirty little secrets."

"I've wanted to but she's been reluctant, or maybe afraid to come," Alan told her. "She just keeps saying that maybe she'll come someday but not now."

"Maybe she's just not into spankings, not everyone is you know," Suzanne said calmly.

"I realize that. I don't expect her to take part in anything; I told her that, but she could still come and meet some of the members," Alan said softly. "After all, you guys are all my best friends."

"Then have a party outside of the club and invite some of us. We'll get to meet her on safe, neutral ground." She gave him a devilish grin. "We may even be on our good behavior."

"I'll set it up." He hugged her and walked away. "My birthday is coming up soon. Thanks Suzanne, you're a genius."

"Remind me to give you a birthday spanking," Suzanne said as she walked away, "a really good one."

"As if you would ever forget," Alan laughed.

Suzanne went to find James. A middle-aged woman had just spanked him, and as usual, the smart spanking had made him horny. He handed Suzanne a glass of Cold Duck, and slapped her on the butt.

"Having fun?" he asked, grinning at her.

She sipped the Cold Duck and grinned back at him, "I sure am. How about you?"

"Well, if I was getting a few more kisses, it'd be even better."

He leaned over to kiss her. The kiss was both tender and passionate. "Why is it, all I really want to do right now is take you home to bed?"

"Are you tired already?" she asked, with her blue eyes full of mischief. "You must be getting old."

"If we were near a bed right now, I'd show you how old I'm not getting." He leaned closer to her and whispered in her ear, "I'd make love to you until neither of us could walk."

"Why go home?" Suzanne squeezed his hand. "When there's several bedrooms right here. Maybe we can find an empty one."

"Good idea, let's go get naked." He led her into one of the empty bedrooms and locked the door.

They made love passionately and tenderly, reaching a shattering orgasm together. While they were basking in the afterglow, he gently, almost too gently, spanked her slightly pink buttocks. He finally gave her one hard slap on each cheek and asked her to spank him.

She gave him a sound spanking, in spite of the fact that she kept getting distracted by the urge to kiss and nip his smooth, taut buns. She kept it up until he rolled her over onto her back and took her into his arms, sliding into her once more with a smooth hard thrust. They made love again, fast and hard. This time, as they lay side by side catching their breaths, he cuddled her gently and kissed her forehead and her silky, long hair.

"Suzanne, I love you very much. I can't picture my life without you," he said, kissing her gently. "Will you marry me? I need you beside me, always."

"I love you too, and I want to spend my life with you," she replied, tears forming in her eyes. "But I have a few questions to ask before I give you an answer."

"Okay, fire away, what are they?" He sat up in the bed, still holding her tightly.

"First, just to be sure, what kind of marriage do you want? Conventional? Open? Do you know what I mean?" She was afraid that she hadn't phrased it very well.

"I only want to have sex with you. I mean, I want a

monogamous marriage, I'm pretty traditional in that way. But I do want to keep active in the club. Does that make any sense?" he replied.

"Perfect sense. We can spank or be spanked by others but we save our lovemaking for ourselves. It works for me." She hesitated, and asked him shyly, "My next question is, how do you feel about kids?"

"I want kids, lots of kids, the sooner the better. I love kids," he paused, then continued seriously, "but we have to keep this side of our relationship away from them. Let them find their own sexual nature, when they're old enough."

"Would about seven and a half months be too soon for the first kid?" she asked shyly.

For once, James' usual intelligence failed him as he questioned before he thought, "But doesn't it usually take nine months?"

Suzanne laughed so hard that she almost fell off the bed. James finally realized what he had said, and what Suzanne's question had meant and started to laugh too. He was a wreck, hugging and kissing her, and laughing until his sides hurt and tears ran down his face.

Finally he got control of himself. "Does this mean yes?"

"Yes!" Suzanne kissed him again, and they just laid there, side by side. "It's a good thing you popped the question tonight. I'm really glad you proposed before I told you about the baby. It makes it seem even more special."

"So am I, my love." He kissed her hair. "Now you'll always know that I'm not marrying you just because of the baby, the little one's a bonus." He leaned down and kissed her still flat belly.

They held each other and talked for a long time, planning their future. The club outside was forgotten as they enjoyed the feelings that come from making a life changing decision like the one to get married.

Meanwhile, out in the main room, the spanking play continued. Sherry followed Suzanne's example and got a spanking from Santa Jerry. Her lover, Clayton, used a wooden paddle on several women with real severity before he got a whipping from a large, middle-aged woman. Sherry watched as he bent over a rail and the middle-aged woman used a riding crop to give him a long slashing and painful beating. When he had all he could handle, he raised himself up. He pulled up his charcoal gray slacks and traded places with the woman. Using the same crop, he gave the woman a tremendous cutting whipping across her fleshy buttocks. He had just finished when he turned and saw James and Suzanne emerging from the private bedroom.

"What's up you guys? You look suspiciously happy," he asked, noticing their broad smiles.

"Let's go over to the bar, we have some exciting news we'd like to share with you," James said.

They wandered over to a table near the bar, and James got them all some champagne.

"Okay, what's up?" the ever-curious Sherry asked. "What's this exciting news?"

"We just decided to get married," Suzanne answered, her face glowing with joy.

"Great! Congratulations to both of you!" Sherry hugged James, and then Suzanne.

There were hugs and kissed all around. Clay gave Suzanne a friendly, warm hug and kissed her cheek. He topped it off with a friendly but smart slap on the ass.

"Careful!" James yelled, almost in a panic. "She's pregnant."

"As if I haven't been getting spanked all night long," Suzanne laughed.

"But that was before I knew about the baby," James was chagrined. Sherry and Clayton were still laughing as the other couple walked away.

Suzanne and James returned to the main part of the party, not really participating in any more spanking games, but visiting with friends and sipping their champagne. They found Jerry and told him their latest news.

"Hey, that's not fair!" Jerry hugged her. "I saw you first."

"Yeah, but you already have a beautiful wife," James reminded him, "and a long happy marriage."

"Jerry, we want to go home, in fact we have a cab waiting outside. Will you tell Edna for us? And give her our love?" Suzanne asked him.

"I sure will, Lass. Congratulations." The older man kissed her cheek.

"Goodnight," Suzanne said as they left.

Jerry remembered back to when he and his wife Edna were expecting their first child. They had seven children now, and four grandkids. Jerry went over to her. She was sitting in a corner talking to one of the other women in the club.

Edna was an attractive lady, plump and gray-haired, with a wise, sweet face, and gentle brown eyes. She had on a plain cranberry knit dress that managed to show off her still beautiful figure. To look at her, a stranger would never believe that she had been spanked fairly harshly by at least three different men at the party, or that she had used a whip with a great deal of vigor on a young stud of about twenty-three. She looked up and saw the grin on her husband's face.

"Let's go home, dear." He smiled at her with love in his eyes. "I want to be alone with you."

"It's about time, Mr. Claus; I have a list of things I want from Santa." She kissed him. "It's a very long list." She took his arm and they walked to the door.

"Santa will try to give you everything you want," he said, sliding his hand down to pat her affectionately on her ass as they were walking to their car. "And he's got a surprise to tell you about when we get home."

"You mean the surprise about Suzanne and James deciding to get married?" she said. "Even from across the room, I could tell what all that hugging and kissing was about."

Jerry opened the car door. "Spoilsport."

"Does she already know that she's pregnant? Or didn't she say?" Edna asked.

"She knows," Jerry said, kissing her before helping her into the car. "How did you know?"

"Jerry, the girl's got that glow. I guessed it two weeks ago." She watched him walk around and get into the car. "There's only one thing I've never figured out."

"What's that, my love?" Jerry asked.

She nudged him gently, "I've never figured out if that special glow came from the sheer joy of being pregnant, or if it was from just morning sickness. Has she told James?"

Jerry laughed as he started the car and drove away. "Sure she did, right after she accepted his proposal. But enough about them, tonight I have big plans for you and me."

"Your wish is my command, Santa," Edna teased her husband with a quick wink, "once in a while."

For an older couple, they sure had a busy night when they got home. Jerry was so impatient that he undressed his wife and made love to her right there on the living room carpet still wearing the top part of his Santa suit, before they went upstairs. Many of the club members would be shocked, and even somehow encouraged, to learn that a couple of Jerry and Edna's age made love more than once that night and in more ways than one. They should have known; how did they think Jerry and Edna had those seven kids?

Chapter Seven

The Amazing Maze

Just after the first of the year, the special event Sherry had been so curious about finally arrived. The event was called The First Annual *Amazing Maze*, an entirely new kind of event put on by the members of the Paddle Club, and open to outsiders strictly by invitation only. The invitations were issued with a great deal of caution.

The event featured a maze set up like the ones in a fun house at a carnival, with some mirrored walls and some seemingly solid walls, except that these mirrored walls would actually move around and trap the couples until they performed required acts on each other.

Once a couple paid the admission fee and entered the maze, there was no way out. No one could escape without sampling all the tender delights of the maze, "tender" being the operative word. Each couple was forewarned, to disobey the voice they heard was to court true disaster, i.e., being stuck in the maze with no way out, and no food or bathroom in sight.

The standing policy in the Paddle Club was that spankings, paddlings and whippings could be done in public while all other sexual acts were kept private, behind closed doors. Sometimes that policy was set aside for events like this one. Some of the things they would be told to do were sexual in nature, very sexual, but they would only be asked to do them with their own partner.

Sherry and Clayton entered the maze and followed the path around to the left. They heard something slide softly. Turning around, they realized that they were already trapped in a small enclosure made up of mirrored walls. Seemingly from nowhere, a woman's voice came to them.

She said, "Okay now, both of you take off all your clothes.

Leave the clothes here, neatly folded please, and go through the opening. Remember, in this maze there are several places where a wrong turn can mean repeating part of the maze. That can mean a little extra pleasure or extra pain, or even a little of both."

As soon as they both had their clothes off a small opening appeared in one section of the wall. They had been instructed to go through it so they did; so far so good.

Shortly they were trapped in another small area. The same female voice said, "Give the lady one good, hard swat on each side of her butt. Then continue down the path."

It didn't seem like any big deal but when Clayton did it, the sharp swats on her rounded ass sounded like a gunshot in the small space, although they didn't really hurt very much. CRACK! CRACK! Immediately an opening appeared in one wall.

The couple followed the only path open to them. As soon as they rounded a corner, they saw a bed and heard a slight sound coming from behind them. It was the wall being moved. They were once again in a small room with no way out. There was a velvet box sitting in the middle of the bed.

Again they heard the voice, "The gentleman will lie on the bed. The lady will use the vibrator on him until she is told to stop."

Clayton lay down on the bed. Sherry paused for a moment to admire his muscular, well-built frame, and then she turned on the vibrator and began to use it on him. At first she avoided any contact with his genitals, using the vibrator to trail slowly down his chest. Finally, she used it carefully and gently on his balls and his large well-formed cock. His erection was full and hard. All too soon for Clayton, when he was in the grips of a tender torment, the voice told her to stop.

"I'm sorry but you'll have to move along now, there are other people waiting," the female voice said, not sounding sorry at all. "Please move along."

Sherry and Clayton traveled a little farther along the path of the maze. They found another bed. This time Sherry was instructed to lie on it and Clayton was ordered to use his mouth on her pussy. Climbing onto the bed, he knelt between her legs. He slid his arms under her legs, lifting them onto his broad shoulders and reached for her full breasts with his hands. He flicked the nipples with his fingers and rolled them between his thumb and forefinger. Slowly, he lowered his mouth to the soft, red-gold tangle of curls and made his way down. He began to eat her hot pussy with deep, firm thrusts of his soft, wet tongue. The wall opened too soon again. This time leaving Sherry writhing in the throes of unfulfilled, aching arousal. Following orders could be frustrating as hell, she decided.

"I really liked that room!" Sherry protested, her amber eyes wide with excitement. "I wanted to stay at least a little while longer."

"Sorry my dear, but you only have a short time at every stop. Who knew the *Maze* would be so popular?" Again the voice had an edge of laughter that made her sympathy sound more than a little phony. "We should have planned better."

"Oh, oh! This looks like another trap to me!" Sherry exclaimed.

There was a wooden chair sitting in the middle of the mirror lined path. From somewhere off in the distance they heard a smacking sound and a long scream.

The disembodied voice commanded, "Madam, be seated and have the gentleman lie across your knees. You both know all too well the position I mean. Give him a good hard, and I do mean hard, spanking! Right on his very tight, very well defined butt! Remember, I want your hand to hurt as much as his ass!"

"I'm glad you like my butt!" Clayton quipped. "Someday I'd like to get my hands on yours!"

Clayton placed himself on her lap and she gave him as long and harsh a spanking as she had ever given to anyone. She put all the force she had into her blows until his firm round butt turned a bright red and her hand throbbed. It was a long time before the voice told her to stop.

"Funny how we had plenty of time for that!" Clayton muttered rubbing his smarting butt. He heard an almost ghostly laugh.

The wall moved and the couple progressed down the twisting path. They came to a fork in the path and took a wrong turn,

56

ending up back at the same wooden chair. Following orders, Sherry spanked Clayton again as hard as she could. He got off comparatively lightly this time however because her hand was already sore! They proceeded with caution around a corner and came to a padded whipping bench.

"I hope this one's for you," Clayton told her with a tight, evil grin. "I owe you one!"

"Indeed sir, have her pick a number out of the bowl without looking at it, then strap her down," the voice instructed and paused for a moment before asking, "What's her number?"

There was a small table with a fishbowl filled with small white numbered balls on it and a box next to it. Sherry closed her eyes and took a ball out of the bowl, then handed it to Clayton.

"Six!" he called out, and then strapped her to the bench. He was told to open the box; in it was a tawse.

"Six with the tawse, well laid on!" came the order.

The tawse was an extra wide, thick leather strap. It was about fifteen inches long and four inches wide, with the last five inches divided into four sections. Clayton swung it fast and hard. It landed with resounding cracks on her ass, causing her to scream with loud full-throated screams. It also caused several dark red, blotchy bruises. When the sixth blow was given, he unstrapped his bruised darling and they waited for the wall to move.

They went around several corners until they were boxed in again. It was at a padded bench. The same padded bench. This time Sherry pulled out a 1!

"Hardly seems worth the effort," she remarked carelessly, bending over.

"I'll make sure it's worth it," Clayton stated firmly, leaning over to kiss her ear. "Very sure."

His words sent a shiver down her spine. This time he didn't bother to strap her down, he just hit her with the tawse as hard as he could, once. It hurt worse than any single blow she had ever felt before. She screamed.

"Hurt, love?" the voice called out, laughing gently. "So sorry dear but the best, or the worst, is yet to come for both of you."

As they walked along the path, Sherry said casually to Clayton, "Payback will be hell!"

They came to a dead end.

The voice commanded them, "Sherry, drop to your knees and give him a hand job. I want you to fondle his cock and balls until I tell you to quit."

"Did you say payback would be hell? Or heaven?" Clayton grinned.

Sherry complied, enjoying the task of fondling his large cock, almost as much as Clayton enjoyed the sensations it caused. She fingered his balls and stroked his hard smooth cock, building up speed and pressure as she went along. Clayton stood with his legs spread apart, and slid his hands into her hair, grabbing it but not too roughly. He threw his head back and closed his eyes, savoring the sensations she was causing. Once again the voice stopped the action with Clayton just short of orgasm.

"ARGH!" he uttered as the voice sounded again.

They heard the now familiar ghostly laugh. Clayton finally recognized the laughing voice, even though it was distorted to sound more ghostly.

"Suzanne! I should have known it was you, you witch! I'm going to get you for this!" he shouted into the air, waving his fist. "You're not playing fair!"

The laugh was the only reply he received.

When they were told to stop the next time, the room had a bed and a box with another vibrator in it, this time for Sherry. She lay on her back, and Clayton used the vibrator to send her into a state of shivering rapture. He concentrated on her clitoris, stimulating it much more than her vagina. It was great, even though her ass was still sore! The voice permitted her to come to her wondrous orgasm before telling Clayton to stop. Women have to stick up for each other, after all.

"Suzanne, you're playing favorites!" Clayton complained.

"I'm not; we were just getting a little backed up. There are so many couples ahead of you," she protested.

"Sure, and cows fly!" he muttered.

The couple once more moved on down the road. Several twists and turns later they wound up back at the bed. Once again Sherry was on the bed; this time she got on her hands and knees, and Clayton stood behind her to use the vibrator. He reached up between her legs to use the vibrator, driving her wild. Sherry quickly reached another orgasm, with the vibrator in Clayton's skillful hands. They went on.

Another corner, leading to another padded bench, and another table with a box. This time, the box held a pair of dice. "Roll those dice, sir! Call out your number!"

"Twelve!" Clayton called out.

"Not real lucky sir, are you? You'd better avoid Las Vegas. Over the bench. Be sure to strap him down tightly, Ma'am. He may try to squirm." Clayton reluctantly laid himself over the padded bench, remembering the promise she had made about payback.

When he was strapped down the voice called out again, "Look in that small chest."

Sherry opened the chest and found several birch rods.

"Twelve with the birch rod, and make them harsh!" the voice ordered.

Sherry did her best to give him the full measure of the birching, making the rod swish in the air. SWISH! "ARGH! AH! AH!" Clayton shouted at each cut, with good reason.

"Umm," Sherry murmured, gently stroking his red, hot butt, "revenge is sweet."

"Remember my love, there's plenty more yet to come. I might get a little revenge myself," he warned.

After the birching, they went through a series of turns and wound up, once again, at the bench. This time he got ten. Again, she strapped him down tightly, and again, she was extremely severe with the rod. She slashed his butt over and over, sometimes landing on previous stripes. In fact, she drew a little blood. Throughout the whole birching, Suzanne laughed openly.

Shortly after that, he got his revenge on Sherry. At the next stop, he was told to take her over his knees and give her a really hard spanking. The only problem for Clayton, at that particular moment, was that he didn't want to sit down. Not at all! He put all his strength into spanking her bottom with hard, hearty blows.

He kept his rhythm by singing all the while he was spanking her. "I've been working on the railroad, all the livelong day!"

When she stood up Sherry said, "Beat me if you must, Sir, but please, please sing on key!"

"I'll have you know that I have a terrific voice!" Clayton said with a huff.

"Then use it next time," Sherry said archly.

The distant voice laughed again. It took several turns for them to come to the next stop. It gave both of their aching butts a rest, in a way. At least neither one received any new bruises.

Chapter Eight

More Amazing Fun

They came to a bed and the omnipresent voice called out, "On the bed, Sir. Hands and knees!" When he was in position the voice continued, "Put that dildo up his butthole! Work it in and out, and work it hard!"

Clayton opened his mouth to complain but thought better of it and reluctantly got into the required position.

"Why the hesitation, Sir?" Suzanne's voice floated in the air.

"Damn it Suzanne!" Clay almost shouted then he dropped his voice almost to a whisper. "No one's ever put..."

"Not anything?" Suzanne's voice was soft.

"No!"

"Then you'll find out now what it feels like. I'd bet you've done it to someone," Suzanne was laughing. "Who'd have guessed? A virgin."

"I will kill you; just you wait and see," Clayton threatened.

Sherry found some lubricating jelly on the bedside table in little individual foil packets and used it before she gently inserted the dildo into Clayton's asshole. She slid it in and out firmly and quickly, without being overly timid or gentle in her manner. Clayton's asshole was tight and he felt quite a bit of pain, but he still enjoyed the sweet torture.

As they got up, Suzanne asked softly, "How did you like it?"

Clay shot her the finger. Sherry followed instructions and put the used dildo into a plastic bin, then opened the drawer and placed an unused one out, ready for the next victim.

The next two stops were very pleasurable for both of them. At the first, Clayton had to kiss her ass, tonguing it all over. He really put all of himself into it, teasing and arousing Sherry to the point where she wanted to drag him to the floor and make love

61

to him then and there, Suzanne or no Suzanne! This time she was ordered to move on before she reached her climax, and as she got off the bed she was so frustrated she really wanted to strangle her best friend!

Then Sherry had to use a feather and an ice cube to tease and provoke Clay. First, she tied him to the bed on his back and then she trailed the ice down his muscular chest. She paid particular attention to his nipples, bringing them both to hard, taut buds. She iced his navel and then placed the ice cube very carefully on his pubic hair, very near his painfully erect cock.

Abandoning the ice cube in its intimate position, she picked up the feather. She used it to tickle the soles of his feet and brought it up his legs slowly, until at last she began to tease his balls.

Finally with the ice in one hand and the feather in the other, she turned her attention to his cock. She drove him out of his mind. Right up until the voice ordered her to stop, as usual just short of his orgasm. It took Clayton an almost superhuman effort to drag himself off the bed and continue on down the path! Again, they heard a few moans and screams off in the distance, and closer to themselves, the ghostly-disembodied laugh.

They both began to wonder, was this a trend or the calm before the storm? When they came to the next trap they found out. There it was, a padded whipping bench.

Sherry was ordered to roll the die, and call out the number before she allowed herself to be strapped down over the bench. Sherry rolled a lucky 7, and after putting herself into position, took seven very hard cuts of the birch. Clayton put strong wrist action into each cut. Every slash made a whistling sound as it went through the air. SWOOSH! Every slash brought a scream from Sherry. She was loud! Her screams broke the sound barrier. Strangers on the street, who had no idea that the *Maze* existed were looking around for fire trucks and ambulances; she was very loud indeed!

It was Clayton's luck that it was Sherry's turn to use the tawse on him next. His luck that he pulled number 15 from the fishbowl. This would not be a good day for him to go to the racetrack. When you're hot you're hot, but the common phrase was taking on a whole new meaning of its own on his butt! She used the tawse with a ruthless efficiency, giving him the fifteen blows, with slow, heavy swings. She was careful to make sure that none of the blows were any softer or easier than the rest.

Again there were two easy stops in the maze. For the first, he was ordered to suckle her full, round breasts. He sat on a chair in front of her and she straddled his legs, lowering herself until her breasts were level with his mouth. He laved her nipples with his tongue, moving from one to the other. He began to suck on her right breast, causing her legs to buckle so that she had to lock her arms around his neck to keep herself in place. He moved to the left breast, giving it the same tender treatment.

Then, for the next stop, he was ordered to lie on the bed while she tongued his buttocks and asshole. She threw herself into the work, using her tongue and teeth all over his backside and moving slowly closer to her target. Finally, she did something she had never done before and used her tongue to tease his anus. Clayton was wild! Good stuff! Enjoyable! Even better, painless!

Surprisingly, Sherry was a little squeamish about using her mouth on his anus, but the voice, when it asked her to stop, told her to look into a small drawer on the stand beside the bed. In the drawer, there was a supply of small trial size bottles of disinfectant mouthwash. Sherry laughed, but she put the small bottle to good use.

They had a long twisting walk to the next trap. They turned a corner and then stopped in their tracks as they saw what awaited them: side-by-side whipping benches and two large men, impeccably dressed in white tie and tails. There were no visible, shall we say, weapons. The scene was so unexpected that they both laughed, but only for a split second.

When they were both strapped down next to each other, the men stood behind them and began to swat Sherry and Clayton alternately on their butts with some long, heavy, wooden paddles. They got six swats apiece, each one laid on with a heavy, hard swing.

Six swats may not seem like a very large number, but on already red, sore asses, they were enough. More than enough. Sherry and Clay were untied, and with shaky legs they set off down the path again.

Once more there were fairly easy stops for both of them. She was ordered to get up on the bed, on her hands and knees. He lubricated the dildo and worked it up her ass. The dildo was large and long, and as it had with him, caused her some degree of pain, but the sensational orgasm she reached was worth it.

Then, at the next stop, she knelt down and gave him a hickey on the inside of his thigh. It was such an easy task that it hardly seemed worth it until she made it a very intimate and sensuous experience, letting her mouth stray from his thigh to his abdomen, his balls and his erect cock.

During the next twisted section of the maze, Sherry remarked, "It's a pattern you know, a couple of easy stops, a long walk and then, a killer stop!" They turned a corner, "Oh, my God!"

Just as it had been at the last hard stop, the scene was set up for side-by-side whippings, with two big men waiting. But these huge, burly men were not dressed in formal tuxedos. They were dressed in black with leather masks, just like the outfits worn by medieval executioners!

For the first time, the pair could see what implements were there to punish them, a pair of cat o' nine tails. No shit!

"Milady, pick a number." One of the men held out a bowl and Sherry picked out a numbered ball that she handed to him. It was a 5. "Milord, Milady, kindly put your hands into the manacles on the walls!"

In a few short seconds, they were both chained up and hanging from the walls. Clayton quipped, "At least it's not our butts again."

It was the last joke he made as the lashes of the cat bit into his back! These were not the prop whips used by some S & M enthusiasts, that sting without causing marks or any real pain. Each slash of the cat caused both real pain and welts when it landed on either one of them. They both fought the restraints.

They struggled and screamed, until it would have seemed to an outsider that they were in some rather weird competition to see who could squirm the most or scream the loudest. They both got the full measure of their five strokes! The lashes certainly caused welts although, due to the skill of the men, they didn't draw any blood.

Again they worked their way along the maze, and once again the stops were quick and painless. Sherry was told to suck his nipples. At 5'4" to his 5'11" her head came to a point just a little above his chest. It was easy for her to bend her head just enough to lick and suck his chest until both his nipples were in tight little buds.

A little farther along Clayton gave her a big hickey on the inside of her slender thigh. Like her, he had trouble staying focused on his prime objective with his mouth so near to her succulent cunt. He licked and sucked her legs and thighs and began to move towards the tender, moist center of her femininity.

Suzanne's voice cut in and she sweetly stopped him. They were told to move along. Her exact and very ladylike phrase was: "Move it or lose it, you two horn dogs!"

Sherry waved a fist into the air, yelling, "Damn you, Suzanne!"

They were both jittery walking along the maze. If the pattern held true to form, they were coming to a killer trap. They were surprised when it wasn't. Sherry gave Clayton two hard swats, one on each side of his ass, trying in vain to find a spot of skin that wasn't red already.

"This'll be the bad one!" she said, but Clayton was ordered to kneel in front of Sherry and finger fuck her cunt. He put himself into the task with his usual businesslike efficiency. He gauged exactly how his touch was affecting her by the expression in her eyes. He built her almost to a climax and then backed off, prolonging the sensations. The ever-present voice told them to move along leaving Sherry hanging again.

"This time it'll be painful for sure!" Clayton predicted, but instead Sherry was ordered to kneel in front of Clayton and take his cock into her wet, willing mouth.

She licked the whole area, slowly building his excitement. Then and only then, she took his cock into her mouth, using her hands to fondle his balls at the same time. She began to suck his cock and balls. Once again, the voice told her stop just before he came. Once again, Clayton made a silent promise to himself; he was going to get Suzanne back if it was the last thing he ever did.

The next stop was another pleasant one; Clayton used a feather and ice to tease Sherry. His approach was different from hers had been when she used the same items on him. He tickled first, using the ice only as a sort of place mark between her legs. Finally, he asked her to spread her legs as far as she could and he used the feather on her pussy. Suzanne, the unseen voice, in the spirit of sisterhood, let her reach her orgasm this time. Then she directed them to continue through the maze.

They went through a long series of twists and turns before they finally reached a trap.

The voice spoke to them, "It's almost over, my dears. Wait for the door to open and then run like hell! Ready now? ONE! TWO! THREE! GO!"

The door opened into a long hallway that was lined with about a dozen people holding long switches. As the couple ran the gauntlet, the people holding the switches used them with lots of vigor and absolutely no mercy!

When they got to the end of the gauntlet, they both had stripes on their arms, legs, backs and asses. They ended up in a small area, where they were told to wait. They were each given robes to wear. They opened the door and found a guide waiting for them. The guide led them into a small private room.

The room had a large bed, a washroom, a closet with their clothes in it and an ice chest. Inside the ice chest were two very cold bottles of champagne and a bottle of lotion for use on their sore bottoms.

The voice came over the air, "You two did really well. Did you have fun? I just want you to know that this is a private room. There is no one who can see or hear you. Stay for as long as you want to, and enjoy," Suzanne paused. "Please just remember to change the sheets. Oh, and you are more than welcome to replace two of the people working in the maze so that they can go through it, if you want. You'd be amazed at how many workers this thing needs."

In spite of their throbbing buttocks they put the room to good use. Clayton hesitated for a moment when he realized there were no condoms in the room but at Sherry's fevered nod, he plunged ahead. They made love wildly and passionately, then cuddled for a long time in each other's arms.

"Why don't we change these sheets and go out to volunteer. I feel like whipping someone's ass!" Clayton finally suggested.

"I feel like whipping Suzanne's ass!" Sherry agreed.

"She'll get hers, after she has the baby," Clayton promised.

They put on their clothes and went out to find one of the guides. They were put to work on the gauntlet, using the switches on the people still going through the maze. It was fun to whip someone else's butt for once. Suzanne had told them to be severe and they were; after all, they had learned to obey her voice!

Chapter Nine

A Warm Circle Of Friends

Soon after the *Maze*, Alan threw a birthday party for himself. It was a just a quiet dinner party with dancing on his patio afterwards. The only Paddle Club members he invited were James and Suzanne, Clayton and Sherry, and of course, Jerry and Edna. His new girlfriend, Sharon, was a slender blond with blue eyes and a shy manner.

She seemed to warm up to the group from the club. Even to the point of taking Suzanne aside and speaking to her about Alan. She told Suzanne that she was very concerned about Alan because he belonged to some sort of sex and torture club.

"I can't even imagine my gentle Alan hanging around with those people." She giggled nervously. "That's why I was so glad to meet you. Maybe you can help me get him away from those... those... "

"Weirdoes?" Suzanne suggested, smiling.

"It works for me," Sharon said firmly.

"That might be a little hard for me to do." Suzanne looked at Sharon with compassion. "You see Sharon, we are the weirdoes." She paused when Sharon gasped. "James and I, Sherry and Clay, even Jerry and Edna. We came here especially so that you could meet us and find out that we aren't really so strange. In fact, he threw this party just so we could meet you."

"But you're all so pleasant and normal, how could you be involved in something so, um, nasty?" Sharon shivered.

"How could Alan? Let me tell you more about it. That way you'll be able to really understand Alan." Suzanne crossed her heart, solemnly. "I swear I won't try to talk you into anything."

Suzanne and Sharon talked for a long time. When they were finished Sharon had promised to think about coming to a party.

She said she would even consider participating, just once, to give it a fair try.

"Since it's so important to Alan." She whispered, "I really do care for him, you know."

"He cares for you too." Suzanne smiled. "He's not going to let you get into anything disgusting and terrible."

By that May, which was almost five months after the *Maze*, Suzanne felt bigger than the proverbial beached whale. She and James just made a token appearance at the club. In fact, the past four or five times they had been to the club were token appearances.

It was not unusual for one of the female club members to be pregnant; the members of the club tended to join in pairs, and other than their club activities, most of the members were usually very devoted to their lovers or spouses. The only unusual thing at this party was that now there were two pregnant members. Sherry wasn't as far along as Suzanne, but she definitely was beginning to show. Most people guessed that she became pregnant on her honeymoon, which was about a month after the *Amazing Maze*. Suzanne guessed the date a bit differently; she had a feeling that Sherry got pregnant on the very day of the *Maze*. She knew a secret that the other members weren't in on, she knew there were no condoms in that bedroom, at least, not until Sherry and Clayton left the room.

It was a very hot night for May, and many of the members wore very skimpy outfits. Things like spaghetti straps and shorts were the uniform of the day for most of the women. James was dressed casually in jeans and a blue polo shirt, yet as usual he looked cool and comfortable but still neat and well groomed. Suzanne, however, was in a pink floral tent of a dress, and any attempt at looking or being cool and comfortable was far behind her. Like all women at this stage of their pregnancy, she had forgotten just exactly what her feet looked like. She only knew how sore and swollen they were.

The other members came up and gave Suzanne a kiss on the cheek and a pat on the stomach. They gave James a sly wink. So many of their friends kept asking her when she was due that Suzanne felt like she should have the phrase "in about a month, now" stenciled on her forehead, just to save them the time and effort of asking.

Sherry, in a cute lime green maternity dress, joined Suzanne who was sitting on the sidelines with Sharon, watching the action and not actually participating in any of it. She really didn't need to wear a maternity dress quite yet, but she was proud of her first pregnancy and still enjoyed showing off the slight belly. That'll change soon enough, Suzanne thought, when she gets bigger and her feet start to swell.

Sherry and Suzanne drank the cold, fresh milk the bartender had especially for them, and put their tired feet up. Sharon had an iced tea. They relaxed and watched as their husbands and Alan walked around the room and greeted friends, joining in the fun.

James was with Edna, the older lady holding his arm and whispering in his ear. After a few moments, the odd couple walked over to one of the padded benches.

"Are you sure it's okay for me to keep you from your wife so long?" Edna asked, glancing over at Suzanne. "I want a good long paddling, but not very hard, all right?"

"It's fine, my dear, and I promise to give you a good paddling. You just tell me what you want, and I'll do it." He smiled gently at her. "But you have to return the favor. I need a good, long, and in my case, hard whipping with the cane."

"You got it, Bud." Edna smiled and laid down on the padded bench, reaching back to raise her red and white print dress up off her buttocks.

James paddled the rowdy older woman right on top of her plain cotton underwear with a round wooden paddle, knowing from experience that she didn't like to have her underwear pulled down. It was not a very hard spanking at all but it went on and on.

Finally, Edna had enough. She stood up and straightened her dress. Then she reached out and took the cane James had beside him.

"Thank you, James," she said with a gleam in her eyes and a blush on her face. "It's your turn now, so bend over."

He dropped his jeans, revealing that he was not wearing any underwear, and laid down on the bench.

"Naughty boy!" Edna exclaimed, pretending to be shocked, which she wasn't. She may like to keep her own underwear in place but she loved looking at men, especially naked men. She whipped him much harder than he expected.

She was a strong lady, and not afraid to make good use of a bamboo cane. He held off as long as he could then he stood up and pulled up his jeans, carefully zipping them, in spite of his rather large erection.

"Thank you for the canning, it was really wonderful." He bowed to Edna and kissed her hand.

"Anytime, you nasty boy, anytime." She reached up and fondly patted his cheek. "I think I'm going to go find my husband and ravish his body."

"Edna, my love, you give me hope for the future." James hugged her warmly.

"By that, you mean you hope that you and Suzanne are still as kinky and sexy when you're as old and gray as Jerry and I are?" Edna grinned. "Gee! Thanks a lot."

"Edna dear, neither you nor Jerry will ever be old; gray maybe, but never old, and that's my hope for Suzanne and me." James kissed her gently on the cheek.

James started to turn away from the bench when he was stopped by Annie, the only black woman in the club.

"Could I have a taste of that, please?" she asked. Her light brown eyes were filled with amusement and for a moment James wasn't sure what she was looking at, the cane in his hand or the rod poking out the front of his pants.

"Sure, Annie, just get in place," James answered, realizing that she meant the cane.

When she had draped her long, slender body on the bench and raised her long black skirt, he whipped her. He used medium force, not as soft as on Edna, but not really hard. He hadn't whipped her before; in fact he really didn't know her very well because she was still a fairly new member. He wanted to make sure it was just right for her. She gasped a few times before she stood up and thanked him in a low, sweet voice. There were traces of tears in her eyes and a soft smile on her lips.

Right in the center of the room, a slender, pretty blond was being tied up by an older member. He had a long gray ponytail and a definite sparkle in his eyes and he expertly wound the long soft rope around the blonde's hands, waist and legs. Watching him work was fascinating, as it was an art in itself. She was seated in a chair, facing the back of it, with her skirt pulled up and her bare bottom hanging well out over the edge of the seat. She kept up a lively commentary as he tied her. Telling him which ropes were too tight and which were still loose. She seemed to be enjoying the attention thoroughly.

Finally the older man was done. The young woman was tied, immobile and ready for the cane. He caned her with efficiency and enthusiasm. Soon, another member came up to him with a comment and he turned to speak to the man. With a touch of devilment shining in her eyes, the blond scooted the chair around and back so that her bottom was actually under the edge of a nearby table. Laughter sounded around the room.

His conversation finished, the man turned his attention back to the blond. He pointed the cane at a clear spot in the center of the room. "You managed to get to the table, now you can get back here where I can cane you properly."

Pretending reluctance she complied. The laughter in her eyes gave her away, and she was rewarded for her impertinence with a lengthy and harsh caning. When it was over, some of the members applauded.

Over at the other bench, Clayton was holding court. He had a much more stern and businesslike appearance than James did. He was even dressed in his favorite charcoal gray suit pants, and a long sleeve shirt and tie. His only concession to informality was that he had left his suit jacket at home, loosened his tie and rolled up his shirtsleeves. The rolled up shirtsleeves looked ominous. He seemed stern and forbidding but the members who were better acquainted with him really knew it was all a sham, as he had a wild streak a mile wide.

Clayton was administering whippings with a school cane in a strict but efficient manner. He didn't really look at the bottoms he whipped, not even to notice if they were on a male or a female. He just kept the line moving. Everyone who got into his line knew the whipping they got would be hard, fast and unemotional. Alan was the last in line.

"Okay, I quit." He finally dropped the cane. Suddenly the facade dropped and he was laughing and breathing hard, a wide smile on his face. "Now you ingrates, who's going to volunteer to whip me?"

He got more volunteers than he needed, and they were eager to whip him as hard as he could possibly want. James walked over to watch the action for a minute, noticing that Clay was getting some pretty severe treatment from some of his former victims.

James decided to go join the wives. About halfway there, one of the youngest women in the club stopped him. She was a tall and tan platinum blond named Nancy. She had long, silky hair and vibrant, green eyes, enhanced by colored contact lenses. In a flirtatious manner, she asked him for a whipping. James looked across the room and met Suzanne's eyes and wisely decided to decline.

"Sorry Nancy, I think Suzanne needs me," he mumbled.

"She keeps you on too close a leash; I can never get near you," Nancy pouted.

"Even Suzanne gets jealous if I spend too much time with someone as pretty as you," James said diplomatically, before adding, "and that's odd because I think she's the most beautiful woman in the world and even if she weren't, I love what's inside her. Her intelligence, warmth, humor, heck even her soul are even more beautiful than her face and figure."

"I wish someone felt that way about me," Nancy said softly.

"I'm sure someone will, someday," James said softly, and then he went over to join Suzanne.

"I'm sorry, but I don't just like that woman," Suzanne said when James had joined her at the side of the room. "I think she's a walking mantrap."

"I know and I think I've handled it." James smiled. "I told her she was pretty-"

"Oh, that'll discourage her." Suzanne was sarcastic. "Good thinking."

"And I told her that my wife was the most beautiful woman in the world, inside and out."

"Really?" Suzanne's eyes were shining.

"I meant it, you know." James kissed her tenderly.

"I know." She smiled. "I think you're the most handsome, and perfect man in the world too."

"But when I first walked over here you sounded jealous," James observed.

"I know, and in a way I am jealous," she admitted, then explained, "Not because I think you'd ever do anything with her but only because that bitch can see her feet. But, and remember I told you this, she's after your body and she's not going to get it."

"How can she help chasing me?" he asked with false modesty. "Just look at me; even you said it. I'm perfect."

"Yeah, a perfect jerk." She punched him in the arm. "I told Jerry once, when he complained that you got all the pretty girls, that I would be the last pretty girl you'd ever get. I meant it then and I still mean it."

"When did you tell him that?" James was curious.

"The night we met, when we got out of the car at your house. Remember when he complained that you got all the pretty girls and I whispered my answer in his ear?"

"I was dying of curiosity, of course I still remember it." James sighed. "Do you mean that my fate was sealed already?"

"I meant that your future happiness was assured already and you better remember it, buster." She punched his arm again.

James pretended to fend off blows. "Help! Help! She's beating me!"

"So who do you want us to help?" Sherry interjected, laughing. "You or Suzanne?"

Sharon, who'd been watching this interplay, along with everything else going on at the party joined in the warm laughter. Suddenly, Suzanne stopped laughing; she got a funny look on her face and her hands slid down to rest gently on her bulging stomach. Sherry noticed immediately but James kept on kidding her. Clayton and Alan walked over to join the group. At last the men noticed Suzanne's strange behavior.

Finally, Suzanne spoke, "It's probably nothing at all, James. But I think we should go home."

Once they were in the car, Suzanne asked him, "Are you sorry that I made up my mind to marry you from the first night we met?"

"My love, I was only wondering what took you so long." James stopped for a light and leaned over to kiss her gently. "I think I knew from the phone conversation. I was sure the moment I met Michael."

"Why?" Suzanne turned to look at him.

"There was no way that creep was going to keep me from having a wonderful, kind and sexy lady like you. I've never been sorry about one moment of our life together." James kissed her.

"What about tonight, are you sorry we had to leave so soon?" she asked curiously.

"No, I'm not. It was probably a mistake for us to go to the party tonight, anyway," he said with a rueful grin.

"Why?" she asked curiously.

"Just what usually happens at club parties; all that whipping gave me an erection," he said, pulling into the driveway. "Of course, there's no way you and I... " he trailed off looking over at her swollen stomach.

"Don't be silly," she whispered with a wicked grin. "I still have a mouth."

Chapter Ten

Ooh Baby Baby!

As it turned out, the strange feeling Suzanne had at the club party was not premature labor but just a false alarm. Her due date was still five weeks away. Finally, four weeks after the party she really went into labor.

She'd been having strange aches and pains all day but they were fairly mild and not regular. She refused to worry about them, but was awoken in the middle of the night with the first of her hard contractions. She waited through a few of them without waking James. Finally, realizing that they were coming at regular intervals and getting harder, she woke him up.

Suzanne calmly checked her overnight bag to make sure she had already packed everything she needed. She called her doctor's exchange and told the night operator she was on her way in, then quickly showered, dressed in a loose, but very comfortable, faded blue housedress, and settled back to watch as James ran around the house in a panic. She put an end to his madness when her pains got much harder and closer together, coming at five minute intervals.

She told him, in a firm, gentle and ladylike manner, "Cut the crap, Bozo, and drive me to the hospital, now. And I do mean right now!"

James answered with the words every married man knows all too well, "Yes, dear. Right away, dear."

He managed to gather his wits just enough to take her small overnight bag in one hand and her arm in his other, and help her to the car. He forgot his car keys however, and left her standing on the street next to the car while he went back to search for them. Of course, he had managed to leave them in the house and lock himself out. He turned and gave Suzanne a foolish, helpless look and saw her dangling her own car keys in the air.

She laughed affectionately as he got in and started the car. "God, it sure is a good thing I love you so much." She reached over and patted his red cheek.

There was one small thing about her pregnancy that Suzanne still hadn't told James. One secret. She wasn't sure if he knew about it or not because she asked her doctor not to mention it to him. If James was watchful and smart enough when he went with her during her ultrasounds he would know; if not, he had a surprise coming. The odds were in her favor because James had bad luck when it came to her doctor visits.

He always seemed to get tied up with problems at his business every time he planned to go to the doctor with her. He had either missed her appointments completely or come in late.

It frustrated the hell out of James but it really worked well for Suzanne, at least as far as keeping her secret went. She hoped he would be as happy as she was. She wanted to surprise him and really hoped he'd be ecstatic about it.

Luckily, in the process of concentrating hard enough to drive safely, some of James' nervous energy abated and at least a small amount of his normal intelligence returned. They pulled up in front of the hospital and he helped her out of the car, leaving her bag behind long enough to take her inside and get her into a wheelchair. He spoke to the admitting clerk, giving her his insurance information and all the other necessary data. He signed endless forms. Then he went to retrieve the overnight bag and move the car out of the special parking spaces labeled "for admitting only."

While Suzanne was being examined he paced and checked his watch, wondering if he should call all the people on his list. Since it was almost six in the morning, he decided to wait until about seven to call anyone except his parents who lived about a three-hour drive away. Most of their friends went to work around nine, so at seven they should probably be waking up.

His Mom came on the phone, her voice filled with drowsiness that vanished instantly when he said the magic words, "I know I woke you up but Suzanne's in labor, Mom. It could be anytime."

"We'll be right there, at least as soon as we can," she told him. "Give Suzanne our love."

"What about me?" he asked sounding slightly left out.

"You've got the easy part, dear. All you had to do was make love, zip up your zipper, wait, drive her to the hospital and remind her to breathe. Men!" his mother said dryly before she hung up.

The doctor, a gray-haired woman in scrubs, came out and told him it would be a little while longer. She had a nurse take James back to the labor and delivery area. They left Suzanne in his tender, loving care. He sat beside her and held her hand while Suzanne was having pains every five minutes. She yelled and cussed him out every time the pains hit her, and breathed deeply and tried to relax when they eased up.

During the short period between labor pains she was her normal, serene and loving self. In the grips of her contractions, however, he began to fear for his life! For one thing, he knew for sure he would never get the feeling back in his right hand.

Her pains got closer and James used the phone next to her bed to call Sherry. He asked her to call Jerry and Edna. Then he called Suzanne's mother who lived across town. Suzanne's father, Joe, was dead. He had been killed in a car wreck when Suzanne was eighteen.

Suzanne gasped and managed a small laugh as she rested between pains. "I see you've spread the word, Paul Revere, now are you ready to be invaded? They are all going to come, sooner or later."

"I just hope this one," he patted her belly and kissed her, "comes soon."

At that moment another pain hit, the hardest so far, Suzanne was ready!

The doctor came in, checked her briefly and said, "All right, this is it."

What followed next was a progression from hell to heaven, and into total shock for James. The birth of their daughter was very hard for him to watch at first. He didn't like seeing Suzanne in pain, and was too scared and excited to relax until he actually saw the tiny head emerge. His fear faded and he became proud and exhilarated as he watched the rest of her small body come into the world. She was perfect and healthy; also slimy and all kinds of strange colors until the nurses cleaned her off. She was beautiful.

The doctor held the tiny baby up for Suzanne to see but she didn't let Suzanne hold her. A nurse took her off to one side. James looked over to watch the nurse working with his daughter and something strange registered in a corner of his brain. He turned back to ask the doctor about it and he was completely taken by surprise! Suzanne was in labor again. A short time later a tired, stunned, but thoroughly happy James went into the lobby to find their friends and family.

"They're here; twin girls and they are both healthy and beautiful," he announced with a wide smile. "They both weigh about five pounds, give or take a few ounces. Suzanne's fine. Would you believe it? She never even told me she was having twins. I never even guessed until I realized they had two bassinets in the delivery room, and that was after the first one was born."

James' mother, Elizabeth, a trim gray-haired lady of fifty with a merry grin hugged him, crying. Then his father, Frank, a dapper gent of sixty hugged him so tightly James was worried about his ribs. Aw heck, he thought dazed, at least cracked ribs would go well with his shattered right hand. Both father and son had happy tears in their eyes. Then he accepted hugs and congratulations from Suzanne's mother, Mary. She was in her late forties and was a shorter version of Suzanne with her dignity, sense of humor, jet-black hair and vibrant blue eyes. She was dressed in a peach knit dress and looked really smashing.

"I'm gonna have to spank that girl because she never even told me, her own mother, that it was going to be twins!" Mary was a little surprised when a couple of Suzanne's friends laughed so hard they almost choked on their coffee. "Hey! I'm just kidding."

Everyone quickly assured her that they knew she was joking. Everyone decided to go to the nursery to see the babies together, as a group. After that, they were going to go out to brunch to celebrate. They took the new grandparents along since they would have to wait until a little later before anyone could get in to visit Suzanne. James went back to his wife as he knew his parents and his mother-in-law were all in good hands.

"You better rest up, my dear. The whole group is visiting the nursery and then they're going out to brunch, but that's as long as I can hold them off. Then the invasion begins." He kissed her gently. "Have I told you yet that I love you?"

"Not lately," she smiled wearily, "but I think I already knew." A nurse brought in the twins.

"So what do we name these two?" James asked.

"Darned if I know." She yawned. "That's your job. Surprise me."

"How about Mary and Elizabeth?" they heard Frank say. They looked over and saw the group gathered in the doorway. "That's what grandmother's are for."

"We weren't going to name the baby after any of the grandparents because we were afraid we'd hurt someone's feelings," Suzanne explained.

"However since we have two, one for each new grandmother, I think it's a good idea." James kissed her gently. "What about you?"

"I love it," Suzanne said tiredly. "Which is which?"

"We can decide later." James kissed her. "After you get some rest."

James' father walked over to Suzanne and took her hand. "I want you to know, Suzanne, that if you ever have a son, I expect you to name him after your father. He missed a lot by not seeing the fine woman you've become; he deserves that tribute at least."

"He would have loved James and you too," Suzanne mumbled sleepily.

"Hey you guys, Suzanne's tired. I thought you were going out to brunch," James said.

"We decided we couldn't wait," Edna said. "But we have already stayed too long, and Suzanne needs her rest."

Frank kissed Suzanne's forehead and left the room. One at a time, the new grandmothers and their friends came in and hugged and kissed Suzanne. They hugged James too, but gave most of their attention to the two small baby girls. They all kept their visits very short. James' parents insisted he join them for brunch and let Suzanne rest. Seeing Suzanne's drowsy nod, he went along.

Chapter Eleven

A Nosy Neighbor Gets Hers

James and Suzanne missed the next Paddle Club party which was held shortly after the birth of the twins, but by the following month they were ready to go. Suzanne felt a little uncomfortable because she hadn't gotten her shape back to where she wanted it, but James assured her that her natural beauty had very little to do with her figure, and he was right. Besides he believed that it took a real pig of a man to belittle a woman about the changes in her body when she had given him a baby or in Suzanne's case, twins.

Suzanne picked up Sherry and Clay on the way to the party. James was tied up at work; he would meet her there later. Sherry was now about six months pregnant and beginning to feel large and clumsy. However, she looked cool and comfortable in a floral print maternity jumper.

When they pulled into the familiar driveway, there was a woman standing on the steps of the clubhouse that neither Sherry nor Suzanne knew. She seemed hesitant and a little hostile. She acted as if she wanted to knock on the door but was too shy or afraid. She was dressed in a black dress with white flowers printed on it and a white linen blazer. Her brown hair was short and looked as if it had been styled by a top-notch hairdresser. Both her make-up and jewelry were impeccable yet still understated. She looked as if she was dressed for a business meeting, but her attitude didn't fit with her appearance.

As Suzanne and Sherry walked up the steps, she introduced herself, "Hi, I'm Carol Dupree, and I live in the neighborhood," she began.

Suzanne wondered what she meant by that because the nearest house to the clubhouse was almost a half-mile away, but she greeted the woman. "I'm Suzanne and this is Sherry. We haven't seen you here before. What brings you out to our club?"

"Well," Carol hesitated, "I live in the new subdivision, Pinecrest Homes. I've only lived here a short time but I've heard rumors that this is some kind of a weird sex club and frankly, I'm concerned about it because I have kids. I thought I'd check it out and find out the truth before I tried taking any action to get the club closed down. I want to be fair."

"Well Carol, let's sit on the porch and talk about this," Suzanne replied calmly. Her naturally regal and serene attitude gave her an edge over the other woman. "I really do appreciate your approaching us openly before trying any other actions. Although you do realize that we are outside the city limits, don't you? In fact, we're in another county from your house."

She and Sherry sat down in some of the comfortable chairs on the porch. When Carol joined them, Suzanne decided to play hostess and asked, "Can I get you something to drink?"

"I don't drink liquor," Carol said pointedly, looking at Sherry's obvious pregnancy.

"Why do you assume we meant alcohol?" Sherry asked quietly, her usual humor suppressed. "I mean yes, we do have a bar and a liquor license, but we also have almost any juice, soda or designer water you can name and, of course," she rubbed her belly gently, "milk."

"I'm sorry, that was rude of me, wasn't it? I shouldn't be making judgments about you without the facts." Carol apologized but it was a very stiff and insincere sounding apology. "I would enjoy some lemonade."

"I'm not really sure you should be judging us at all, Carol. After all, what right do you have to judge us?" Sherry said quietly. "But we'll answer your questions anyway, since we have nothing to hide."

"Clay, this is Carol," Suzanne said as Clayton came walking up to join them on the steps. "Carol, this is Sherry's husband, Clayton. Would you be a dear and bring her some lemonade? And orange juice for me. What about you, Sherry?"

"Milk," she made a face, "but don't ask me to like it."

While they were waiting for Clay to bring the drinks Suzanne took the direct approach with Carol. "I don't know exactly what you've heard but in a way you are right, as this is a sort of sex club. It's probably not what you're thinking, but it is a sex club."

Clay brought the drinks, including a beer for himself. He surprised Sherry with a chocolate milk shake instead of just a plain glass of milk. He handed out the glasses and then sat on the clubhouse steps, leaning gently against his wife's knees.

"Thanks Clay, you're a doll." Sherry was pleased with his thoughtfulness.

Suzanne took a large swallow of her orange juice and spoke quietly. "Clay, Carol has heard some of the nasty rumors about us and she's a concerned citizen. I told her we were, in fact, a sex club."

"Subtle, Suzanne, real subtle." He grinned at her, took a long drink of his beer and met Carol's eyes. "But, fair's fair, we are a sex club of sorts. We don't do the things you're probably worried about though."

"How do you know what I'm worried about?" Carol asked, a touch of acid in her voice. "What could you possibly know about me?"

"As much as you could possibly know about me," Clayton paused. "Let me guess. You are probably thinking about promiscuity, group sex or maybe even orgies. Then there's liquor, drugs, increased crime, maybe even prostitution, plus the effect of all those things on the community, especially young impressionable kids, and the added problem of sexually transmitted diseases, especially AIDS. Is that about it?"

Carol nodded, "How did you know?"

"Because," Clay said gently and firmly, "we worry about those things, too. The truth is, we don't have sex with anyone but our own spouses, or if a member's single, his or her lover. There is no swapping going on here and we don't have group sex, or public sex. Drugs and alcohol? We don't do drugs, and anyone who does is kicked out of our club immediately. We also have an excellent system for making sure no one who leaves one of our parties is driving under the influence of any drug or alcohol. Anyone who has a DUI after one of our parties is not only just plain stupid but they are also immediately kicked out. Sexual slavery? No one is exploited here or asked to do anything against his or her will. Everything is consensual. Child molestation? Not only would any member with a hint of any those proclivities be kicked out, but also reported to the police. No one under the age of twenty-one is allowed to attend, drink or take part in anything even remotely sexual. In fact, if someone is immature for their age, we'll keep them out too. We have members who are doctors so we get free health exams frequently. Bad for the community? We try to keep our activities out of the public domain. We very generously support several local charities, and we will kick anyone indulging in illegal activities out on their rears. Anything else?"

"That sounds good, but how can it be a sex club if you don't have sex?" Carol was puzzled.

"We like to keep certain things private, just like you probably like to keep things that you and your husband do in bed private. It's not because we think there's anything wrong with it but because it is our private business," Suzanne replied. "Just exactly how did you hear about us, and what did you hear?"

"A man that my husband does business with told us that he attended a party here once without knowing what the club was about. He said he was subjected to being tied up and whipped, and that the members here took turns raping his fiancée," Carol said shivering at the thought. "He said after that night, he never saw his fiancée again. He thinks she may have been murdered."

Suzanne looked startled but she had to ask, "Was this a mean-spirited little jerk of a man, late thirties, named Michael Martin?"

"Yes," Carol replied. "Was he telling the truth?"

"In a way, as he saw it, he probably was," Suzanne replied, her eyes on Carol's face. "But not the way I saw it because I was the fiancée. He knew exactly what the club was about and he didn't just attend a party, he applied for membership. After all, he wanted to see me get tied up and whipped."

While Suzanne paused to think, Clayton said quietly, "Go on

and tell her, if she'll keep it to herself."

Carol added, "If I can, without compromising my sense of morality, I will keep your secret."

"Okay, here's the truth as I saw it: Michael and I had been involved for quite a while and for most of that time I thought I loved him. He said that he had heard about a special club for spanking enthusiasts. He begged and pleaded with me to try it, even though I had never been involved in anything like that before. I realized later that he just wanted to see me hurt and degraded, but that's not what happened... "

Suzanne told Carol all about her initiation to the club, how she met and married James, and explained briefly what the club was about.

She finished with, "You see, Michael had it all wrong. We're not really a BDSM club, we're more into role playing and spankings than inflicting or receiving real pain. Also, in our club everything is strictly voluntary, and we make sure there's no victimization. Heck, even clubs that feature more BDSM are based on consent. There is no group sex and certainly no rape. That's why Michael was not allowed into the club, they could tell from the first that he was filled with rage and cruelty."

While she was talking, Clay had brought out another round of drinks.

"You may think we're strange, maybe even abnormal, but I don't see how immoral we can be if we're monogamous," Sherry said. "And we all care very deeply about each other."

"If you're telling me the truth, I guess you're right." Carol admitted, "I don't see the attraction, but I don't see anything particularly sinister about it either. Except for one thing, how can a woman who's pregnant be involved in this? Aren't you risking your baby's health?"

Sherry laughed, "I'm just here to visit with some friends and catch up on the latest gossip. Believe me, I won't be involved in any risky business. You have to see what we're like to understand so come on in, we don't really have anything to hide." She invited Carol inside, and then saw a man approaching. "Who's that?"

"My husband, Abe." Carol introduced him.

He was tall and heavy, with a rough face and a guarded expression in his eyes. He didn't seem to be at all Carol's type; his appearance was blue collar to her white collar.

Carol told him, "We've been invited into the club, as guests."

"But you have to try participating just a little, to see what it's like," Clayton said.

"By participating you mean... " Carol flushed as her voice trailed off.

"By participating, I mean you must try a light spanking, nothing really painful, from both sides, giving and receiving." Clayton was firm, "Or you won't learn a thing about what we're like and what we do. And, if you don't participate, you'll just make the members feel uncomfortable. Sherry can skip participating because we all know her but you're a new face, and we don't want you to embarrass our regulars. So come in and join in the group or go home, it's up to you."

Carol moved off a little and spoke quietly into Abe's ear. They walked back over to the group and Carol spoke. "I'm scared, but Abe's willing to try it so I guess I can, too. As long as I can leave whenever I want."

"Come on then." Clay held the door for the group. "I think they're going to start a fast game of musical chairs, as silly as that sounds."

There didn't seem to be any games starting up, or anything else going on when the group got into the main room of the clubhouse. All the visitors could see was a group of friends sitting quietly and talking at various tables around the room. There was soft rock music playing somewhere in the background. A buffet table was set up beside the well-stocked bar. Abe and Carol were invited to have something to eat. The food was varied and superb; there was everything from vegetarian pizzas to prime rib, and desserts from plain vanilla ice cream to elaborate torts. Everything in the room seemed so normal and yet somehow very elegant that Abe and Carol both felt foolish,

87

embarrassed and just a little bit disappointed.

That was, until they saw a young man hand a paddle to a woman and after dropping his pants, bend over a table. The woman began to beat him with the paddle using slow hard strokes until he straightened up and pulled up his pants. Abe and Carol both went pale, and Carol seemed to shiver whenever the paddle landed on the young man's bare butt. Neither Abe nor Carol was prepared for the young man to take the woman over to a bench and tie her up. He gave her a much harder beating than she had given him. She squirmed and yelled throughout the paddling. The young man kept it up until the woman yelled, "Stop."

"Notice that he stopped immediately when she gave the word," Suzanne pointed out.

The young man turned around and found two other women waiting behind him. As Abe and Carol watched in amazement, the young man beat them too.

There was a pause in the music, and then the strains of classical music filled the room. Another man in his mid-thirties bent over a chair with his bottom bare. While he was being caned he sang an operatic aria, and sang it very well.

"He has an excellent voice doesn't he?" Clay whispered as he rose from his chair.

Clay left the table and walked over to talk to some friends. Jerry and Edna walked over to join the group. After introductions were made, Suzanne dragged Jerry off to a padded bench and had him give her a fairly smart whipping. She took advantage of getting Jerry alone to tell him that the new couple was two "concerned neighbors" who had dropped in to find out what was up. She also mentioned that they had agreed to participate in the club. Jerry took the hint immediately.

As soon as they got back to the table, Suzanne looked up to see James coming in the door. She ran over to greet him warmly then brought him over to the table and introduced him to Abe and Carol.

She explained to the visiting couple, "You'll have to excuse my husband and me; we need to be alone. Sherry, Clay, Jerry and Edna will take care of you. Have a nice time." She dragged her husband away.

After they left Edna said, "Well, I guess the doctor must have said she was completely recovered from childbirth. Remember, she said she had her final checkup today."

"Maybe she just wanted to get him alone to tell him the doctor said she wasn't ready to resume sexual relations yet," Jerry suggested with a wink.

"Yeah, my love, and cows fly." Edna smiled. "That girl is just plain horny."

"Well, if my second favorite woman in the world is going to abandon me for her own husband, I guess I'll just have to take care of Carol here." He reached over and took Carol's hand, gently pulling her out of her chair. "Come along, Miss, it's time for you to get a spanking," he said with a merry grin.

Carol sputtered, "But... but... "

"That's right dear, I'm going to spank your butt," he said cheerfully. "Abe, paddle my wife's ass for me, will you please?"

Jerry led Carol away, over to a comfortable wooden straight-backed chair. He sat down and pulled her across his lap, ignoring her squirms and protests. He slid her skirt up and spanked her gently until she stopped wiggling around. After a while, she seemed just to lie there and take it. Jerry slid his hand gently over her silky underwear and hose before he spanked her a bit harder.

When her bottom was nicely warmed up he stopped and let her up. "It's customary to thank someone for spanking you, girl." He grinned at her.

"Thanks a lot." Carol sounded sarcastic.

"Did I hurt you?" Jerry asked. He dropped his character and was suddenly serious. "I mean really, did I hurt you?"

"No," Carol admitted weakly.

"Better luck next time," Jerry said, grinning again. "Now go and get that paddle and use it on me, please. And don't be easy on me, I'm used to it, okay?"

Carol got a paddle and returned to find Jerry bent over with his pants down, waiting patiently. She paddled him for a long time and fairly hard too. Finally, he stood up and thanked her.

"Now let's go see what your handsome husband is doing with my wife." Jerry slid his hands around her waist and squeezed her affectionately. They arrived back at the table to find Edna using the paddle harshly on Abe, who didn't appear to feel it very much.

She looked up at Jerry, faintly insulted. "He refused to give me a spanking. He said I looked too much like his mother. His mother! He enjoyed watching you spank his wife though, even if he won't admit it."

"It just looked kind of funny, watching her squirm around," Abe said quietly, "and I could tell she wasn't being really hurt."

"Maybe he'd be more comfortable spanking someone closer to Sherry's age, but not, of course, pregnant," Jerry suggested.

"He's never even spanked the kids at home," Carol added. "He's tenderhearted, I guess."

"Well, if he is, he is. We don't force anyone to take part in our games," Jerry responded to her. "Unless he'd feel better punishing a man."

"What's that mean? Do you think I'm gay?" Abe asked heatedly.

"No, of course not, I just meant that you might be too much of a gentleman to want to hit a child or a woman, but with another man it might be all right," Jerry replied. "We have some members who feel that way and they're straight."

"You may be right." Abe considered the idea. "I could paddle you."

"So go ahead," Jerry bent over, "be my guest."

Abe had just given Jerry about a half dozen half-hearted swats when Clay came over and told them the musical chairs game was ready to start.

"I know it sounds silly but the way we play it is special. Besides, we are silly sometimes; it's part of the fun." Clay explained, "The person who doesn't make it to a chair gets a spanking from the person on one of the end chairs."

There were twelve participants and eleven chairs lined up, six facing one way and five facing the other. Abe and Carol watched along with Sherry as Edna, Jerry and Clay played. It was a good game with lots of laughter, teasing and loud, cracking spankings. By the end of the game, Clay had won. He was laughing as he was attacked by the whole group and tackled to the ground.

When Carol and Abe left, Carol thanked the members for the visit. "I don't think we'll be back, but I don't think we'll try to stir up the neighbors against the club either. It was, umm, interesting."

"We might have some events, regular events that will be open to the community in the future. We want to build up our public image. If we do, be sure to drop in," Clay invited. "As for the other, hey, different strokes for different folks, that's life. It was nice meeting you."

Just as the couple left, Suzanne and James finally emerged from the bedroom. They looked tired, bedraggled and very happy.

"So you two, what's up?" Clay asked.

"Absolutely nothing anymore, finally," James replied with a grin. "Thank heavens."

"My doctor advised me yesterday to abstain for the rest of my pregnancy," Sherry said.

"Gee, Clay, that's too bad," James said with a contented grin.

"Yeah, I'll bet you're full of sympathy," Clay replied.

"Take it easy Clay, it gets worse before it gets better," Suzanne told him. "But it's worth it when you're finally a father."

"It sure is, Clay." James hugged his wife. "It's worth anything."

Chapter Twelve

Jesse's Girl

Jesse finally talked Janine into coming to the club. Most of the members were speculating on just who this mystery woman was. They knew there was a woman who had captivated Jesse. He told them. Repeatedly. He said she was beautiful, full of spice and fire, haughty, but kind. She was also brilliant, according to Jesse. And best of all, she liked to be spanked. Some of the less kind members wondered how a short, slightly pudgy, Hispanic janitor got a woman as exceptional as the one he described but they were wise enough to keep the speculation to themselves.

Walking in with Jesse she looked beautiful and confident, but inside she was shy and nervous. She was indeed as lovely as Jesse had described her but she didn't seem to be haughty. She had a wide, friendly smile. Few of those watching her failed to notice however, that her smile brightened when she turned to speak with her escort, Jesse. She was so engrossed with him; she never noticed the curious looks as she walked through the room on Jesse's arm, meeting people. Jesse smiled to himself as the DJ put on an old song; he whispered in Janine's ear and she began to listen to it. The song was from well before her time, but the chorus got her smiling: 'I wish that I had Jesse's girl, why can't I find a woman like that?' She flashed the DJ a brilliant smile and raised her drink to him.

When she saw James and Suzanne across the room her composure faltered. Her smile wavered just a bit. Jesse's smile widened and he led her straight over to the couple. Short of digging her four-inch heels into the expensive and plush carpet, Janine had no choice but to go with him.

"Hi Jesse, Janine," James said. "It's good to see you here at last. Janine have you met my wife Suzanne?"

Suzanne smiled at Janine. "We've met when I was in the office, Janine. It's great to see you again."

Suzanne kissed Jesse on the cheek and whispered, "Good job!" in his ear.

The four sat at a table and chatted. Janine had begun to enjoy having Jesse spank her but she still felt a bit awkward at the party. She had just started to relax as the spankings got under way.

Janine was a bit distracted by the sight of various spankings that seemed to happen a regular intervals. Sometimes they were bare bottomed, and some over panties. Some were accompanied by protests, and some were met with laughter. Some were just done with hands, but there were a lot of paddles, straps, floggers and canes around the room.

James noticed Janine's distraction. "The one thing you never see here Janine, is anyone who's being abused. Even those who are protesting have the final say in what happens to them. They have safe words to ease things up or stop them altogether."

"But I hear some of them saying 'ouch' or 'stop' so how can that be?" she asked.

"Have your really heard 'stop' and seen it being ignored?" Jesse asked.

"Well no," Janine realized, "unless it was said by someone who was laughing. The 'ouch' wasn't said as a joke though."

"Ouch is not a safe word." The three other people at the table said it simultaneously, all of them laughing.

Finally Janine felt comfortable enough to say it. "I didn't know you were a member here, James. I was shocked to see you outside of work, especially in this um, setting."

"This is where I met Jesse and became his friend," James said with a grin, remembering. "Does it bother you that I saw you at a spankos party?"

"A bit," she admitted.

"But remember, you saw me here too," James pointed out.

"I also can't help wondering," Janine said slowly, "how it is that you seemed not to believe me, at least at first, when I complained to you about Jesse spanking me in the office. You must have known it was true."

"Of course I did." James smiled waiting for her to take the final step.

"You knew and approved of it?"

"Yes." He still waited.

"Before it happened?" She was surprised.

"Yes, I suggested it," James told her. "We normally only spank women who want to play, but that situation seemed to call for some real discipline."

"You suggested it?" She was shocked.

"Of course." James smiled. "You can thank me later, after you've seen the videotape."

"There's a video?"

"But only three people have seen it," Suzanne interjected. "Me and the two brutes at this table. And I didn't get a very good look at it, I was face down over James' knees, getting spanked myself at the time."

"What had you done?" Janine asked.

"Nothing. I was completely innocent." Suzanne smiled. "I don't have to be bad to get spanked, thank God, or I'd go nuts trying to find things bad enough to get spanked for. I'd be in trouble all the time."

"She lets me know in other ways when she wants a spanking, and how hard she wants it," James explained. "And I also let her know when I feel like spanking her, to see if she's in the mood."

"I always am," Suzanne added. "The same with James. He lets me know if he wants to be spanked, but usually that's just here at the parties. At home, he's almost always the top."

"So I was set up?" Janine tried to ignore the picture of James, her boss, being spanked.

"Yes," Jesse spoke up, "but it was your own bad behavior that started it, and that you did to yourself."

"I admit I was a brat."

James had been silent for several moments. "Janine, have you received your results from the bar exam yet?"

Janine's face fell. "Yes."

"I take it from your expression that you failed." He was stern.

"I was so close. I only missed passing by two questions." Janine was devastated.

"Well, beginning Monday, Jesse and I will help you study for the next test," James said firmly. "We'll see to it you pass with flying colors, won't we Jesse?"

"Of course."

"And now," James continued, "I think she should pay a penalty for failing this time."

"Yes, of course." Jesse rose and held out a hand for Janine.

James fumbled through the bag he had tucked under the table and pulled out a couple of paddles and straps. He leaned over to kiss Suzanne. "You're next, my dear."

"I didn't fail the bar!" Suzanne pouted.

"And your point?"

Jesse led Janine over to a padded bench and told her to lay face down on it. He raised her skirt and lowered her panties gently and slowly. He started spanking her with sharp but not really hard slaps, each sounding loud in the now silent room. James stood on the other side of the bench, waiting until Jesse looked up at him and smiled. "Be my guest."

The two men each took a side and spanked Janine with their hands, warming her up, stinging and turning her bottom a bright pink before they each picked up a paddle. They paddled her longer and quite a bit harder than the hand spanking they had given her. Each took a few swipes with the strap, then they went back to the paddles.

"A contest?" James grinned at Jesse.

"Sure."

They began to paddle Janine with fast hard strokes, each playing off the other, each getting faster and sharper. Finally Janine yelled, "Stop!"

They both stopped instantly. They helped Janine straighten her clothes and stand up, and each hugged her warmly.

"Who won?" James asked.

"I'm not sure, we need a rematch," Jesse said.

Both men turned at once, "Suzanne!"

"You men are both outlaws. Jesse and James." Suzanne put herself into position quickly.

When her panties were pulled down it was obvious to Janine that she was well warmed-up; more than that, she had been spanked quite a bit already. The men went straight to the heavy paddles. They raced each other both with speed of the swats and with severity. Suzanne took quite a bit before she stopped things. She hugged both men and summarily dragged James off to the nearest bedroom.

Jesse and Janine socialized, had a couple of cocktails, and ate a great meal; this month it was prime rib. They played a little but not with any other couples. Jesse took her into one of the bedrooms and they made love. Following club policy, they quickly changed the sheets before leaving the room. She had enjoyed herself thoroughly and planned to come with Jesse whenever he invited her. They were among the last to leave and because it was second nature to him, Jesse helped with the clean up, although he would send a crew of his men in to do a more detailed job on Monday. Janine, who had once been thoughtless and careless leaving her mess behind for others to clean, helped him. Of course, it took a few swats for the idea to sink in.

Monday, at the end of the day, when Jesse came in for his customary visit with James, they set up a tutoring session for Janine. They wanted to make sure she passed the bar on her next try. Every day, at the end of the day, they held the sessions.

Janine learned all right. She learned how to study face down across Jesse's lap, with the open law book in front of her on the floor. She learned how to read while being spanked, and hard. She learned how to quote precedents while a paddle came down on her bare bottom. She learned how to argue a case in a moot court with Jesse as the jury and James as the opposing council. She learned that she had to win or be caned. And she learned how to take a caning.

She also learned the law and how to argue under pressure. Passing the bar exam on her next attempt with flying colors, she

received one of the highest grades they had ever seen.
    She got a spanking as a reward.

Chapter Thirteen

A Spanko's Trade Fair

Toni Jackson lay in bed beside her lover Mario Lopez, not sleeping, just staring into the darkness and thinking. She was wide awake, filled with nervous anticipation and more than a little fear about her plans for the next day, Saturday. She hoped that when Mario found out how she was going to spend her day out with her friend Suzanne, he wouldn't be hurt by it or get too mad.

She loved Mario. Just looking at his brown eyes and tan, muscular body gave her Goosebumps, not to mention his lean, almost sculpted face and straight, black hair long enough to brush his shoulders. He was an intense and ardent lover, and a quiet gentle man at all other times.

There was much more to their relationship than physical attraction. They shared a bond of love, friendship and caring that filled her completely. The only problem was that while the physical pull was there, and the sexual fulfillment fantastic, there was still something lacking. She got hot just looking at him. He was a passionate and giving man who enjoyed having sex often. He never failed to please her. So what was her problem?

She thought it might have something to do with a recurrent fantasy she often had, the fantasy of being spanked or whipped! Logically, the thought repelled her with the kind of horrified fascination someone might have watching a poisonous snake crawl across the path in front of him. Logically, she believed that a man who would hit a woman was toad slime. Logically, she believed that anyone who wanted to be spanked was very, very sick in the head. Emotionally, she wanted to be spanked and whipped, but without being dominated or humiliated or even really hurt.

98

She didn't know what to do about it; she certainly didn't feel like she could tell Mario. What if the idea repelled him? What if he thought she was sick? What if he thought her desires were a criticism of his lovemaking, an indication of something lacking, that he wasn't satisfying her? Would he be repulsed? Would he be insulted? Last, but not least, what if he actually agreed to do it? That disturbing thought both terrified and intrigued her.

Finally, the solution to her secret dilemma was at hand. Maybe spending the day at the spanking fair would help her find the answers to her questions. The spanking fair was by special invitation only. It was an event she had heard about from her old friend, Suzanne, who was one of the event organizers.

Toni had lost track of Suzanne after high school when she left the state and went to college in Colorado. It was pure chance that they found each other again. They literally bumped into each other while grocery shopping in the produce section of the large supermarket. When they recognized each other, they quickly put all perishables back, paid for the rest of their respective groceries, placed them into their cars and went to a nearby restaurant for lunch.

Suzanne had made a quick phone call from the restaurant, then she settled back into the plush seat and studied her old friend. Toni was, of course, her age. After all, they had been friends and classmates since kindergarten. She was medium height, about 5'6", and slightly plump, very curvy without being fat, with medium length, curly brown hair and soft brown eyes. She was dressed casually for shopping, like Suzanne was herself. Toni had on blue cotton shorts and a white T-shirt.

"So what's new?" Suzanne asked. "It's only been about seven years since we've seen each other, just tell me everything, that's all."

"Well, I'm a computer programmer, working for a large firm in Irvine. I'm still single, but I'm living with a terrific guy named Mario." Toni smiled widely. "He's handsome, sexy, gentle and kind. I've got to admit it; he's really great."

"Do you think you'll marry him?" Suzanne asked with a grin.

"We'll probably get married soon; we're talking about it." Toni shrugged, "Well for a life story it was short but that's the highlight version, what about you? What's new in the last seven years?"

"The magic question. I'm not working now. I'm married, very happily, to my own really great man. James is good looking, gentle, humorous, sexy and a little kinky and," she paused dramatically, "he's a terrific father."

"You have a child?" Toni was pleased at the thought.

"I have, my dear, twin girls about six months old. Please don't beg, I could be persuaded to show you pictures." She had a small brag book filled with photographs of the babies already out. "I'm just sorry I don't have one of James in here, I left those pictures in my other purse but you'll meet him soon."

"These are the most gorgeous babies I've ever seen; I can't wait to see them in person!" Toni looked at every picture wistfully, happy for her friend, and dreaming about having her own babies someday.

As the lunch progressed, accompanied by several glasses of wine, they began to talk about even more personal things. They fell back into their high school roles of confidants. Toni found herself, almost against her will, telling Suzanne that she had one secret fantasy her lover wasn't fulfilling but she wouldn't tell Suzanne what it was. Suzanne was instantly alerted; she had a feeling that she recognized the symptoms.

She teased Toni by suggesting several odd sexual fetishes. "You want to be tied up? Covered with whip cream? It's a foot fetish? Wrapped in cellophane? Spanked?"

Sure enough, at the last word, Toni blushed. She tried to cover her reaction, but to Suzanne's knowing eyes it was as if it were written all over her forehead. Suzanne began to tell her friend a secret, the secret that she was involved in the planning of a trade fair for spankos.

It was to be like a trade show, for all kinds of spanking paraphernalia, toys, literature, movies and art, she explained, and a few other kinky things. Suzanne also told her there would be some booths set up for sexual games and a bit of experimentation. It would be fun and sexy, but not really sleazy. No one would actually be having sex, either oral or actual intercourse, but there would be several spanking scenarios with actors. Suzanne kept the name of the club secret from her friend.

She smiled at Toni enigmatically and remarked, "I think that you could get a little taste of something kinky, say for instance, a spanking at the fair. Just to see if you'd really like to try it with Mario, you understand. If it repels you, don't ever mention it to him; if not, get him to go for it." She smiled at her friend, "I'll bet he could get into paddling your ass without too much coaxing. It is a much more common fantasy than you realize."

"You figured it out! Witch! I feel so weird." Toni was embarrassed. "And I'd be too scared to ever act out my fantasy! You know that I'm the original super chicken."

"Everything at the fair is strictly voluntary; I will guarantee it in writing. If you don't like anything just say the word and it will stop immediately. And of course, anyone who is involved in the spanking scenarios will be a person who enjoys either giving or getting a spanking, so they won't think you are any stranger than they are." Suzanne paused then asked, "How much wine did we have anyway?"

"Too mush to drive safely," Toni admitted.

"I'm calling a cab," Suzanne said, "and I'll get the car later. Want a ride home?"

"Yes. I think that's for the best." Toni went back to the old topic. "About the trade fair, how do you know so much about this, anyway?" Toni was a little suspicious.

"I can't tell you that or you'll think I'm weird!" Suzanne replied with a laugh and a promise to pick up Toni early the next day. Her cell phone rang. "The cab's here! Boy that was quick."

The two women talked during the cab ride to Toni's house. "See you tomorrow!"

Toni looked back at her friend, "See you."

The next day the two women arrived at the fair very early. It wasn't open for visitors yet but they went on in because Suzanne was part of the planning committee. They visited the few booths that were already set up, looking at some erotic pictures, and laughing at the displays of dildos and fancy vibrators.

"Nothing I need there," Suzanne remarked, "not since I have James. It's too bad you've never met him."

"I still can't believe we lost touch with each other for so many years, and that I missed your wedding." She picked up a large dildo, "Nothing I need here that I don't have at home, either." Laughing, she put it down.

"Ain't love grand?" Suzanne laughed, linking her arm through Toni's.

Toni shuttered when she saw the booth filled with leather outfits, restraints and whips. Did she really want to be here?

Suzanne remarked, "Those leather outfits are just too weird for words!" But she ran her hands down the length of a riding crop. The man running the booth came over and offered to give Suzanne a taste of the crop but she declined. He turned to Toni but she declined too.

With a careless shrug he said, "Tell me if you change your mind." And left them alone to talk.

Toni slyly remarked, "I noticed that you didn't say the whip was weird."

"No, it's beautiful," she answered Toni before realizing just exactly what she had revealed. "Aw gee whiz! Ya caught me! Please don't tell my husband, I'm sure he'd be shocked. Just for that I'm gonna make sure you're the first in line!"

"In line for what?" Toni asked, suspiciously.

"Reward or punishment," Suzanne answered enigmatically.

"But which?" Toni persisted, wide eyed.

"That's for me to know and for you to find out!" Suzanne pushed Toni towards an older man sitting at a small table and asked him to make sure Toni was the first in line when the booths opened.

"Be sure they give her the complete treatment, Jerry. She's a special friend!" She whispered something in his ear, and then turned to Toni. "Wait here! I have to get busy. You just follow the path and do whatever you are directed to do in the scenes. Don't you dare chicken out on this!"

That one sentence alone was enough to make Toni want to run like hell, but not as fast as the final quip of Suzanne's. "I've got a nice, soft pillow in the car for your ride home!"

The little, gray-haired man grabbed her arm just in the nick of time to stop her from escaping. "Come on super chicken, I'm under orders to prevent your escape." He had a merry grin, with a hint of the devil in it.

He slapped her once on the ass, a hard, sharp slap, then he pushed her into the first of a series of small, enclosed booths that formed a sort of horseshoe shaped tunnel. It curved around and ended up almost back at the entrance. As soon as she was in the booth the curtains closed behind her.

Chapter Fourteen

More Kinky Fair Fun

The first booth Toni found herself in was set up to look like an old one-room schoolhouse from the old west in the late 1800's. There were old maps on the makeshift walls, and a blackboard in the front of the room with a series of simple math problems written on it. Across the top of the blackboard, the alphabet was neatly printed in both capital and small letters.

There were only five crude, wooden desks, four of which were occupied by actors playing students; two boys and two girls. All the students acted like bratty kids but they were really people who looked like they were in their early twenties. They were dressed to fit the period of the decor in the room, and most of the girls wore pigtails. At the front of the room there was a stern, older woman dressed as a teacher.

As soon as Toni entered the room the teacher gruffly commanded, "You're late! Sit down, miss! Now!"

Toni quickly plopped herself down at the empty desk. The girl in the front row, a slender blond, wrote something on a slate and held it out to the boy next to her. Disaster struck as she dropped the slate noisily to the floor. She quickly reached down to grab the slate but she wasn't fast enough. The teacher heard the slate hit the floor, turned around quickly and saw the girl pick it up. She hurried over and took the slate from the girl. The girl had written one sentence on it. The slate read, "Old Miss Smith is a mean old toad!"

The teacher dramatically dragged the girl up to the front of the class. She ordered the scared, trembling girl to bend over and grab her ankles. She pulled up the girl's skirt and her frilly slips and pinned them so they wouldn't fall down. She pulled down the girl's plain, white cotton underpants so that her bottom was

104

bare. Then she picked up a long, slender hickory switch and gave the girl six hard cuts across her behind. Each cut made a swishing sound in the air, and each of the cuts caused a long red welt to appear on the girl's pale white behind. It certainly looked real to Toni. It seemed very harsh and painful! Toni squirmed in her seat, horrified and fascinated at the same time. She was sure glad she wasn't the girl being switched. When the teacher was finished switching the girl, she unpinned the girl's dress and ordered her to sit down. The girl sat, gingerly, back at her desk.

Soon after that the teacher said, "Class dismissed!"

Two of the students called to Toni, "Come On!"

They pointed her to an opening in the curtains that formed the walls of the booth, opposite to the one she had entered through. She exited through it.

The second room was more modern. It was decorated to look like a little boy's bedroom. It had posters with football players and scenes from a popular monster movie on the walls. There was a bed with a plain brown quilt that had toys scattered all over it. In the corner there was a baseball, bat, glove and a football.

There was an actor standing in the center of the room who could only be described as a young hunk. He looked like he was barely twenty-one with dark wavy hair, green eyes, bronzed arms and a muscular build. He was wearing jeans and a t-shirt with a cartoon character on the front of it. He was standing there facing the curtains Toni used to enter the room so that he was the first thing she really saw in the room, and Toni was shocked when she immediately noticed that he was crying.

"Please, Momma!" he said when Toni came in, "Please don't spank me! I'll be a good boy from now on!"

As he pleaded, he pushed Toni down into a straight-backed wooden chair, all the while he appeared to be struggling frantically to get away from her. He unzipped his jeans and placed himself with seeming reluctance over her lap.

After a moment he hinted, "Momma, if you really have to spank me, please don't make me wait for it. That's always the worst part!"

He waited for a long moment while Toni sat immobilized.

When Toni didn't do anything but sit there, stunned, he said in a loud, harsh, stage whisper, "Come on! Do it! Spank me! You're ruining a perfectly good performance!"

Toni reluctantly brought her hand down on his white jockey shorts. She raised her arm to strike again, but he grabbed her hand.

He said angrily, "Lady, put some force into it. If you don't, I'm going to forget the script and thrash the living daylights out of you."

She was shaken by his anger, but gave him a fairly credible spanking after that. She managed to put so much force into her blows that her hand started to smart. She must have given him about two dozen slaps when he stopped her by standing up.

"It's okay, Momma, I know I deserved it. I'm not hurt too bad," he sniffled, as he pulled up his jeans, "but I want to be alone for a while." He gave her a grin and a wink then pointed her to an opening in the curtain.

This room was barren except for a full-sized dummy made of canvas and filled with unknown stuffing. The dummy was bent over the end of a padded bench. A man stood off to one side of the dummy holding a riding whip. He was a little older, mid-forties, with salt and pepper hair, slender but muscular looking build, brown eyes, a jogging suit and the manner of an army drill sergeant!

"Good Grief! Do you need this! I peaked into the last room and I can't believe you're such a wimp!" he said, handing her the riding whip. "I want you to beat the shit out of that dummy! NOW!"

Toni quipped nervously, "I didn't know dummies were full of shit."

The man struggled hard but he managed to keep a stern, straight face.

She felt like a fool, but she began to slash halfheartedly at the dummy with the whip. The man turned the full force of his army sergeant persona on Toni. He kept pushing at her, calling her

106

names and insulting her, anything he could do to get her to hit the dummy harder and harder.

Finally he stopped her. "Okay, you're still not hitting hard enough, but at least now anyone that you bestow a whipping on won't actually die of boredom while you do it. Now, I want you to use the whip on me, and make it a lot harder."

He pushed the dummy to the floor, pulled down his pants, revealing a tight, firm, naked butt, and bent himself over the bench. She did her best to whip him just like he had taught her to, but she was still a little squeamish. He kept up his steady stream of insults and nagging, trying to get her to lose her temper and really hit him.

He finally said, "You'll pass, but barely, go on."

He pulled up his jogging pants and directed her out through the opening in the curtain.

The next room Toni went into was made up to look like a little girl's room. It was done in shades of pink, with lacy trim along the small dressing table. There were lots of dolls and stuffed animals spread on the bed, and a white enameled wooden chair standing alone in the center of the room. She felt a strangely familiar sensation as she entered the room because it contained a faint undercurrent of tension. She soon found out why. The actor standing in this room was a fairly tall, stern looking man, in slacks and a sweater. He had brown hair and harsh green eyes.

He looked at her angrily and said, "You took your own sweet time getting here, Missy! The next time I order you to report to your bedroom for a good hard spanking I expect you to get here fast! Really fast! Don't you ever make me wait for you again! Every second I wait will be added to what you can expect to get."

Toni felt a trace of fear run down her spine, along with a sense of disbelief. This couldn't be happening, could it?

The forbidding man sat in the chair. "Well girl, what are you waiting for? Get those pants down, and get yourself over my knees. Now!"

When she hesitated, he bellowed, "You know that you'll just get it harder if you don't do it right now! I haven't got all day."

107

She slowly unfastened and tugged down her tight jeans, blushing furiously. On shaky legs she moves over to the man.

"Well?" he yelled, "What's the big delay? Over my lap! Now damn it!"

He kept the pressure on her, ordering her. That firm commanding voice left her no choice but to obey. Toni felt frozen, trapped in an emotional tug-of-war between fear and desire. Finally she was going to get a real spanking! In a corner of her brain she remembered Suzanne saying it was all voluntary, but this man certainly didn't act like it was. Suzanne had said that she could refuse or call a halt to it at anytime. That may have been true but for some reason, Toni felt like she couldn't take the easy way out.

She laid herself very gingerly over the man's legs. She was shaking so hard that he had trouble trying not to drop her on the floor. He gave her a long, slow spanking on her lacy pink underwear, starting just hard enough to sting a little without causing any real pain.

As soon as she realized that it wasn't going to hurt too much she began to relax, and almost started to enjoy it. Sensing that, the man built up the force of the spanking so that gradually it did begin to hurt. Finally, he lowered her panties and spanked her harder still. It began to hurt quite a bit. Toni realized that she still it enjoyed in some weird way. She enjoyed it a lot! The spanking seemed to go on forever.

When he was done, he pointed out the opening in the curtain and said, "Get out of my sight! Now! I hope that I don't have any cause to do this to you again anytime soon, you bad girl!"

She pulled up her underwear and her tight jeans, and fastened them which made her throbbing, red ass sting even more. She walked slowly through the curtains.

The next area was a barren, empty room. In it was a man with a slender but athletic build, and short, curly blond hair. He was strapped down to a wooden whipping bench. There was a tall, wooden bucket on the floor beside him filled with canes of various lengths and thicknesses.

He turned his head, met Toni's gaze with his soft, blue eyes and said frankly, "Pick out a cane and give me a sound thrashing with it. I mean it, really lay it on hard."

"I can't!" Toni was shocked! "I can't use that on you."

"Why not?" he was openly curious.

"It's too brutal," she shuttered, and then she had a thought. "My God! Won't you be seriously hurt if you're here for the whole day?"

He laughed openly. "We trade off so that nobody gets whipped too much. I won't be here all day. In fact, I'm just filling in right now while the first few people go through because the guy who is supposed to be here is running late. He's having car trouble, can you believe it? You'll probably be the only one who actually gets to cane me. So go on, you might as well enjoy it because I certainly will!" He smiled warmly, revealing a dimple in his left cheek. "Please remember that I'm here as a willing volunteer."

She wanted to do it, she realized with a sense of shock. She was a little horrified by the sudden bloodthirsty streak she felt, but wanted to whip the man, severely. Part of her frenzy was caused by the pain of her still throbbing buttocks encased in the tight jeans, and part of it was that the man frankly said he would really enjoy it. Something hidden deep inside her mind said that if he would enjoy it, and if she would enjoy it, she should go for it. So she did.

She raised up the cane and gave him a slashing cut on his bare buttocks. She shocked both herself and the man with the severity of it, but she kept caning him harshly, never stopping. The cane whistled as it swished through the air. Each cut caused the man to suck in his breath audibly, but he made no other outcry.

Finally, he said, "Enough!"

Toni didn't stop right away, she kept caning him just a little bit longer, only about half a dozen extra cuts, but they were very harsh, sharp cuts. Those last cuts drew some blood. The man gave her a wounded look as he silently pointed the way through the curtains and into the next room.

Toni felt guilty as she put the cane down and walked towards the curtains. As new to this as she was, she knew she should have stopped when he'd asked her to. She also knew that she should never have drawn blood.

Just before she left the room, she turned and said softly, "I'm sorry."

At the last second, before the curtains closed behind her, she heard him whisper softly, "It's okay but just remember payback can be hell."

Chapter Fifteen

Even More Fair Fun

Toni found herself in another small room, this time filled with gymnastic equipment. There were some young women in their twenties and thirties sitting around in a circle on the floor. They were all dressed in leotards and workout clothes of various colors. Most of them had their hair, when it was long enough, pulled back in pigtails or in a ponytail.

In the center of the circle was the kind of padded horse that gymnasts use for the vault. One slender young woman was draped over it, her leotard and underwear pulled down around her knees. She was getting a sound spanking with a gym shoe from a man dressed in gray sweats. He was about forty, a little overweight, with salt and pepper hair, a tan face and brown eyes. He had a big whistle around his neck and one shoe off. It was the shoe he was using on the woman's bare butt.

Toni sat gingerly on the floor and wondered briefly if the coach would spank her too, but she wasn't that lucky. This time she was just another spectator. Since she had now whipped someone and been spanked, she noticed that it felt different to be a spectator. Different from the way it had felt earlier when she watched the spanking without having ever experienced it. Before, she had been fascinated and horrified, now she was excited and secretly aroused. There was a touch of fear creeping down her spine, a rush of adrenaline in her blood, but the hint of fear only added to her arousal. She exited when she was directed to, and went into the next room.

This time it was a prison scene with three female guards. They were all in their mid-forties, and were wearing tan uniforms and black leather boots, with wide black belts. One of the women, a large, gray-haired lady was holding a long, thick, wooden paddle.

A high, crude, wooden table was in the center of the room. As soon as Toni entered the room the other two guards grabbed her and held her. The woman holding the paddle set it on the table and unzipped Toni's jeans, pulling them down to her knees harshly. This time her underwear was roughly pulled down too. Toni was instantly shocked and embarrassed to have her bare bottom exposed to these women. There was not one word spoken aloud in the room.

Toni watched in terror as the woman picked up the paddle and nodded to the other two guards. It was a signal; Toni was quickly pulled to the table and bent over it. Toni struggled but the two guards held her from the front, one pulling on each arm, while the third woman paddled her on her bare butt. The paddling was severe and given with no mercy. It was a series of loud, cracking blows that really stung. Toni tried to take the beating silently, but suddenly she gave a little gasp. A few heavy blows later she yelled, "ARGH!"

The woman instantly stopped paddling her, but when Toni made no further outcry or protest, she began the harsh punishment all over again.

After about six more heavy swats from the paddle, Toni couldn't take it anymore; she gave a yell, "Stop! Please stop!"

The women instantly released her. She pulled her underwear and pants up, then slowly and stiffly walked out of the room. At the exit, she looked back at the three grim and still silent women.

She rubbed her red, throbbing bottom with one hand, grinned softly and said, "Thanks, I think."

She wound up in a sort of barn. A heavy man was bending over bare assed in front of her. He wore a red plaid, flannel shirt and had blue denim overalls down around his ankles. He had his hands braced on a bale of hay and didn't say a word. In a bucket beside him were some short, thick riding crops.

Toni picked out a crop without any hesitation and began to whip his butt with slow, hard blows. She hit him repeatedly, each blow turning the skin of his ass white for just an instant, then almost immediately bringing out a bright red color. The man was silent throughout the whole whipping.

After about fifteen blows he quietly straightened up and said, "Enough."

This time Toni stopped as soon as she was told to. She gave his glowing ass an affectionate pat as she went through the curtain.

The next room was a living room. There was a tan, deep pile rug, a beige colonial style sofa, and several comfortable matching armchairs. Several women were in the room; they were all young, and except for three of them were dressed in nice, bright colored dresses. The three other women were dressed only in their bras and underwear. One of them, a pretty young black woman, handed Toni a paddle. She then bent over in front of Toni, with her hands on her knees.

She said, "For the honor of this sorority, please administer the punishment to this lowly pledge."

Toni gave the woman a single, hard swat with the paddle.

Immediately the pledge answered, "Thank you, Ma'am. May I have another?"

She gave her another swat, and another, and another until she had given her about fifteen, very hard. Toni was directed out of the room.

The next scene was set to look like it was outdoors, in a small clearing. There were five people standing there dressed as pilgrims, three men and two women, all in their thirties. The men had on pilgrim suits, complete with the black hats. The women had on long gray dresses with high starched white collars and crisp white cuffs; they also wore plain white bonnets. The sixth person in the room was a man. He was wearing a white shirt with no coat. He was fastened in a pillory, his head and hands held in wooden stocks, his pants were down around his ankles and his buttocks were bare.

As soon as Toni entered the room, one of the women pointed at her and said, "That's the one! She's to blame! She is a daughter of Satan, just look at the sinful way she's dressed!"

Toni was grabbed by two of the men and put into the stocks next to the man, but her head was put through from the other side so that she was facing his body. She felt her jeans being unzipped and harshly pulled down, followed by her underwear. She could see the five people move into a line behind him, and one of the men started to whip the man with a long carriage whip.

From her position she couldn't see the blows landing on the man's buttocks, but could see and hear the whip slashing through the air. She could also hear the moans of the man every time the whip landed on his butt. It was an eerie sensation for Toni because somehow she knew that she would be next. She was also scared because she was immobilized.

When the first man stopped whipping the male prisoner after about a dozen slashing strokes, he handed the whip to one of the pilgrims standing behind him. This pilgrim only gave the man a single harsh stroke then handed the whip to the next person. It went around the group, each giving the man a single stroke until the final woman gave the man two hard slashing cuts with the whip. The man was left in the stocks, and the pilgrims walked around the room until they were all standing behind Toni. She began to shake but didn't say a word.

The first man took back the long whip and turned his efforts to whipping Toni. He pulled back the whip and slashed it onto her butt with a sideways flick of his wrist. It caused her to feel quite a lot of stinging pain. He gave her just enough time for the stinging to ease a tiny bit, and then hit her again. He gave her six slashing cuts of the whip. Then, as he had with the man before, handed the whip off to the next person in the group, and each of the other four people gave her a single slash of the whip. The last woman paused after giving her the slash and then, after a pause that lasted only seconds but seemed like hours, gave her one last hard slash with the whip cutting severely across both cheeks of her ass. Toni was released from the stocks and pointed towards the exit.

The next room seemed to be some sort of old church or monastery. There were rows of pews and a railing in front. Although there was a raised area in the front, there was no Altar and there were no religious symbols. A woman was on her knees, with her back to Toni, in front of a man dressed as a monk. The back of the woman's long, old-fashioned gown had been ripped open to the waist, with the sides pulled away, leaving her back bare. Her hair was pinned up. She was pleading with the monk. Although Toni couldn't see the woman's face, she just knew there were tears streaming down her face.

The monk was not moved by the woman's pleas for mercy. He made her bend over the rail, and then tied her hands and feet to it. She began to make a loud outcry, sobbing. The monk ignored her screams and protests and began to whip her with a cat 'o nine tails. It seemed to be a long and truly painful whipping. Each blow was a separate and painful torture. The blood began to run freely down the woman's back and ass staining her torn dress.

When the whipping stopped, the monk held out the cat before the woman's tearstained face. She turned her head to kiss the bloody lashes of the whip. Toni gasped out loud when she realized it was Suzanne!

Suzanne said in a shaky voice, "Thank you, Holy Father, for taking your time to whip the sins from me." She gave Toni a wink and pointed her to the curtain.

It was a long hallway this time, ending with a door that said HEADMASTER on it in gold letters. The door opened and a man stuck his head out and said, quite pleasantly, "Come along now, Miss. It's time for your whipping. It'll be all the harsher if you delay."

He looked at Toni sternly. She gasped as she recognized him. There he was, the man she had birched so hard. The man she had kept birching even after he had called for her to stop. No way was she going in there! She wasn't stupid enough to put herself in a position for this man to get his revenge.

He put on a friendly smile as he said, "OH! It's you, Miss. I was hoping to see you again. Don't worry, it's just play-acting, a show. Come on."

He got back in character. "Now, Miss! It's time for me to set your ass on fire. Maybe a taste of the cane will curb your foolish nature!"

He moved quickly and grabbed her arm. He pulled her inside, ordering her to undress from the waist down. Almost against her will, she obeyed, scared and hypnotized. He told her to bend over a padded whipping bench and strapped her down. Although she had been in the pillory, it was the first time she had ever been completely strapped down. She felt totally helpless and immobilized. She also felt very frightened.

"I've been waiting for you, Miss. Normally I use a light cane, but for a really bad girl like you I think the heavy, more severe cane is required." He paused and said with soft menace, "You have a real love of the cane, as I remember it."

That last part of the sentence was personal, not from the script and Toni instantly knew it. This would hurt. Really hurt. He swished the rod in the air a few times; it made a loud, whistling sound that caused her skin to crawl. WHOOSH. WHOOSH. He brought the rod down in a hard swish on her buttocks and the pain was intense. He whipped her again and again.

He disregarded her outcries and calls to stop! The whipping he gave her hurt more than anything she had ever felt. What she didn't know was that for a birching, it really wasn't especially extreme. When he stopped, she had welts all over her butt. He hadn't drawn any blood however, as he was too skilled in the use of a birch rod.

"I guess you've learned your lesson now. From now on, if you stop when I say to, I'll stop when you say to. Never, ever, go past the point of my refusal again!" He gave her a gentle smile. "Even though I secretly liked it."

"I didn't mean to go so far, I got carried away. I'm truly sorry. I felt miserable as soon as I had done it," she apologized, sincerely, and then realized just what he had said. "You say that you liked it?" she was curious.

"Sure, it was great!" he reassured her. "How about you?" he asked as he unfastened her straps.

"It hurt!" she protested.

"But did you like it?" he persisted.

"Yes, I guess I did," she admitted doubtfully, "and as an added bonus, I don't feel guilty about the extra whipping I gave you anymore! Are we all square now?"

"Sure." He held out his hand and they shook, sealing their new friendship.

She smiled at him, then asked, "Have I got welts?"

"You sure do, real pretty ones." He flashed her another smile. "They're some of my best work."

"How in hell will I explain them to Mario?" she wondered aloud.

"Who's Mario? And who cares? What can he do? Beat you?" He grinned. "Not as good as I just did."

She dressed and went through the curtains. She was almost surprised when she wound up out in the sunlight again. As they had arranged before she'd entered the booths, she met up with Suzanne.

Suzanne had replaced her costume with a loose fitting shirt. She told Toni, "I'm taking a break to drive you home. How was it?"

"Suzanne, I can't thank you enough. Not only did I love it but I also don't feel alone, like I'm the only crazy person around anymore. Let's face it, you're all crazy!" she laughed, then suddenly frowned. "But how do I tell Mario?"

"Come here." Suzanne took her to the ladies' room and looked at her behind. "WOW! I see you met my husband, James. Why did he whip you so hard?"

Toni asked, "How do you know it was James?"

"I'm not sure, I just do. A wife knows her own husband's handiwork. Blond, handsome, gentle, a great smile, brutal, a sense of humor and really enjoys his work; does that describe him?"

Toni nodded. She had a serious question to ask Suzanne. "What about you? Aren't you hurt? I saw blood all over you."

Suzanne laughed, "That was totally fake; we have a whip filled with movie blood. I'm kinky, but not that kinky. Now, tell me about James."

Toni explained how she had gotten carried away. She added,

"I'm sure relieved to hear that it was just movie blood."

"James wasn't using any movie blood," Suzanne replied, then she realized what it meant. "Oh, no! You, uh, damaged my husband." She began to laugh uproariously. "I love it! Now I see why he birched you so hard. You deserved it." Suzanne shrugged. "Well, Mario won't even have to guess. Those welts all over your butt are a dead giveaway that you've been caned. Maybe Mario will decide to do the job himself in the future."

"Golly! I hope so!" The women left.

Chapter Sixteen

A Surprise For Mario

Mario was eagerly waiting for Toni when she got home.

"Did you girls have a nice day? Now can I ask where you went?" He was curious because she had refused to tell him about it before they left. "I missed you like hell all day!"

He enfolded Toni in a warm, tender hug and kissed her. Suzanne made her excuses and left quickly; they needed to be alone and she had to get back to the fair.

Toni walked over to sit on the sofa. "Mario, sit down, I have something to tell you. Please let me say it all before you interrupt, please."

It sounded like bad news to Mario but he kept silent.

Toni continued, "First, I love you. I know I should have been able to tell you anything, but I was too embarrassed." She paused; Mario wisely let her gather her wits until she was ready to go on. "I have a secret sexual fantasy that I've never mentioned to you. I felt like it was too weird to tell you about. Don't get me wrong, I love sex with you, you're a fantastic lover. I love you in every possible way. I was just too stupid to tell you my secret desire."

By now Toni was babbling, so she reined herself in. "Anyway, my friend Suzanne belongs to a club, a kind of sex club." Mario started to speak, but Toni continued quickly, "No, I wasn't in an orgy, it was a--"

"Tell me!" Mario demanded, unable to restrain himself any longer, as he was starting to think the worst.

"Spanking! It was a club for people who like to give and get spankings! Please, Mario, let me explain." She told him all about the day. Mario listened in complete amazement.

"I've never tried any S & M, let alone spanking. Heard of it, of course, and thought a lot about it, but never tried it. Let me see your butt."

She blushed and stood up, facing him as she unzipped her jeans. She smiled weakly at him before she turned her back to him and gingerly dropped her jeans down to her feet. Slowly, she slid her silky panties down. She hung her head while he examined her butt. It was still pink, with a few faint bruises, and several darker welts crossing both cheeks.

"WOW! Looks painful!" Mario swallowed, "And you say you liked this? Wanted this?"

"I've had fantasies about it," Toni said quietly. "I wasn't sure if I would really like it."

"And now that it has happened? How did it feel?" He paused, "And did you like it? Keep your pants down while you tell me all about it."

Toni nodded shyly before saying quietly, "I want to say first, there was no sex, not even a kiss involved. I liked some of it quite a lot. The spankings were fun to watch and arousing. Hitting someone else was... hard to get use to, but I did. At one point I sort of got carried away and went too far."

She shuttered, "But knowing that I was going to be spanked, ah, that was scary and exciting, sort of like getting on a really scary roller coaster. Of course, there's also the helplessness and the embarrassment, and the sting. The pain isn't really bad; it smarts and burns, but soon it fades. No one really wanted to hurt me. There was one exception; the welts were caused by a man using a cane, and he was the one I got carried away with. The welts are a payback, meant as a real lesson. To be fair though, he stayed in perfect control. He could have been a lot harsher with me."

Mario got up and paced, thinking, before he asked, "How long is this fair open?"

"Until midnight." It was about two in the afternoon.

"Leave your jeans down and bend over that chair." It was rare for him to issue a command in that stern voice.

When she obeyed, he walked over to stand behind her and

fingered her cunt impersonally, finding out that it was very wet. He unbuckled his belt and unzipped his pants. He took out his large cock and plunged it into her vagina, and began to fuck her wildly. He thrust into her over and over, very hard and fast. He slapped her ass as he fucked her. After he reached his orgasm and she had hers, he pulled his belt out of the belt loops of his jeans and whipped her with it. Just a half dozen slashing cuts, but they were very hard.

When he finished he said, "Good-bye." He started for the door.

"Mario, where are you going?" she asked, nervously.

She pulled up her jeans, ignoring her throbbing butt. She was in a sudden panic; his good-bye had sounded ominously final.

He relented and dropped his stern expression. "To the fair, lovey, to the fair. I have to at least try it, if you like it."

At the door he turned back to her and said, "You might want to be in bed waiting for me when I get home. You know it's where we'll wind up. Oh, and three things you'd better remember from now on: First, I love you. Second, from now on any sex fairs that we go to, we go to together. And third, I get to be the first one to try any new things that you want to experiment with."

"Mario, I'm sorry," Toni was contrite. "I love you. Are you mad?"

"It's okay," he kissed her gently, reaching down with his hands to massage her ass. "But from now on, remember I can manage to give you as many good, hard spankings as you can handle. In fact, in the future, I guarantee it!"

"Mario, wait!" she called after him. "Maybe I'd better go with you. The fair's by invitation only, okay?"

She took him to the fair and led him up to Jerry, who was still on duty at the start of the booths. She gave him Suzanne's name, told him that she had already been through and now her lover wanted to try it. Jerry remembered her well.

"You can go along and watch, if you want," he said, collecting her money. "If it's all right with your man."

"No, thanks. I'll just wait for him at the other end." She didn't want to inhibit Mario.

"Why don't you wait here? I've got an extra seat and I can use the company," Jerry suggested with a warm smile.

"Thanks," she returned his friendly smile with a rueful grin, "but I think I'll stand!"

Jerry laughed zestfully. Shortly after Mario went in Jerry asked her to take over for him for a short while. He showed her the formal invitations, made sure she knew all about the charges, and explained what she should do if someone without an invitation wanted to go in. She listened intently and told him she would be glad to cover for him.

"I know I can trust you with the money and the job, as any friend of Suzanne's has to be completely reliable." Jerry winked at her and left.

He sought out Suzanne and discussed his idea with her. She approved and went to get Edna.

When Jerry returned to his station, after taking advantage of the short break to visit the men's room, he found Toni sitting at his desk.

"I see you can sit after all," he teased her.

"Sure, I'm not hurt," she answered, still smiling a bit ruefully. "Much."

"That's good," Jerry said, with a secretive smile. "That's really good."

"Hi, my love." The woman, whom Toni instantly recognized as the teacher from the one-room school, greeted Jerry. "Is this her?"

Jerry introduced them, "Toni, this is my wife Edna. She's going to take care of you for a while. Go with her."

Toni was puzzled but intrigued. She went with Edna into a separate tent. The older woman gave her a costume, one of the pilgrim dresses and told her to put it on. She kept up a steady stream of distracting chatter while Toni changed. When Toni was dressed, she led her along the row of curtains forming the walls of the booths.

"Why are we doing this?" Toni was puzzled. "I told Jerry I didn't want to watch Mario going through the booths. I thought it would inhibit him."

"But if you watched him going through just one booth that wouldn't inhibit him too much, would it?" Edna asked gently. "Don't you want to see your man get at least one good hard whipping?"

"Yes, I do." Toni smiled as she realized that it was true, she did indeed want to see Mario being whipped at least once.

"Then go in here." Edna peaked through the curtain and waited for a short time. "Right now."

She and Edna went in. Edna whispered to one of the actors playing a pilgrim. They talked quietly for a short time. Edna and the pilgrim grinned at each other and nodded. The pilgrim went over and unfastened the woman waiting in the pillory. He helped her unpin her dress, letting her skirts down.

Toni suddenly realized that she had walked into a trap, but she was too late. The rest of the pilgrims took hold of Toni gently but firmly, and put her into the pillory. She felt her dress being pinned up onto her back.

"A trap! I can't believe I walked into it." She looked at Edna with accusation in her eyes. "No fair. Tell Jerry I said so," she paused, and smiled faintly, "and tell him I said thanks."

Soon, just as Toni was getting good and nervous, the curtains parted and Mario entered the booth. He was shocked to see Toni fastened in the stocks, but before he had time to react he was fastened beside her. He was facing her rump and she was facing his.

The pilgrim leader began to whip her; the blows stung but were not especially harsh. She was still sore and a little bruised from her trip through the booths earlier. Toni acted as though the whipping was as harsh as it could possibly be, squirming and crying out loudly at every stroke. The leading pilgrim handed off the long whip to the others, and as before each one of them gave her a single slashing cut with the whip. The only exception was the last stern faced woman, who again gave her two.

Unlike her trip through the maze, when the first victim was left pilloried while she was whipped, Toni was released and her dress let down before the pilgrims began to whip Mario. There was another change in the routine this time when they handed the whip around; they handed it to Toni last. She was the one who got to give the last two harsh slashes of the whip to Mario. When Mario was sent out through the curtain, they told her to go change and wait for him with Jerry. She thanked them and left.

She returned to her seat by Jerry.

"You are a devious devil, Jerry," she whispered, grinning. "And someday, maybe, I'll get revenge. But thanks for the thought."

"No problem, my dear." He grinned back. "As for revenge, take your best shot. I'm looking forward to it."

When Mario came out at the other end, he was flushed and excited. Sexually excited. He looked at Toni and said, "Let's go home, fast!"

During the short drive home he shot a sideways look at her and asked, "How do we join that club?"

"I guess we can ask Suzanne about it," Toni said, "but let's not worry about it until tomorrow."

"Yeah, I have a feeling we're going to be very busy tonight," Mario said with a devilish grin.

Toni reached over and patted the large bulge in his crotch. "Extremely busy."

Chapter Seventeen

Hot Tub, Hot Sex

Sherry and Clayton both had fun during their day at the trade show, but they had worked in separate areas all day, so they hardly even got to see each other. When the show was over, they dragged their weary bodies home. They checked on the baby, now three months old, paid off the teenaged baby-sitter, and Clayton drove the girl home.

Clayton had spent the day acting as the stern father, spanking his son or daughter. He had also filled in for a short time as the monk flogging a penitent woman. Sherry had been cast as one of the college sorority girls undergoing her initiation for most of the day, but there were two exceptions. She filled in as one of the punished gymnasts for a few minutes. She also filled in for Suzanne as the penitent victim of flagellation, only unfortunately for her, not at the same time that Clay had played the monk. She was very tired, also a little stiff and sore because she had been out of the action for quite a while during her pregnancy. As soon as Clayton left with the sitter, she went into the kitchen to start dinner before going out on the deck to turn on the redwood hot tub to let it warm up.

She checked the intercom they used to monitor the baby's room and made sure she could hear anything their tiny daughter needed. When she checked the water temperature in the hot tub and it was at 105° F, she slid out of her clothes and got in, naked.

Their deck was secluded and she had left most of the outdoor lights turned off. The only lights turned on were a single strand of miniature indoor/outdoor lights, the kind most people put up at Christmas, with all clear bulbs. The deck had several large planters filled with flowers selected more for their scent than their looks, and several dwarf lemon trees. The lemons and flowers made the deck fragrant and relaxing, and the small twinkling lights were beautiful, creating a romantic setting at night.

She had just been soaking in the bubbling warmth for a few minutes when Clayton came home. He brought out champagne in an ice bucket and two tall unbreakable goblets. He opened the champagne and poured it, handing Sherry a glass. He set down his glass and got undressed, then joined Sherry in the hot tub.

"Did you make sure to set the thermostat?" It was something they both checked conscientiously every time they were in the tub.

"I sure did. I plan to take a nice, long soak so I only set it for 105° F," she told him.

They were both aware of how dangerous it could be to drink and soak in a hot tub, especially if the heater just kept making the water hotter and hotter without a thermostat to prevent it from becoming too hot.

Neither one of them could understand how some people turned soaking in the hot tub into an endurance contest, letting their tubs reach 110° to 115° F. Sometimes people would let the water get too hot, drink themselves into a relaxed stupor and practically make soup out of themselves.

Sherry drank her champagne, sipping it slowly. She savored every drop, and when it was gone, she had a slight, comfortable buzz. She put her glass on the deck and leaned her head back against the side of the hot tub. To a stranger she would have looked asleep, unless the stranger happened to notice the slight trace of a smile on her lips, or unless the stranger could see beneath the water.

She took her right foot and lazily played with Clayton's left foot. Slowly she began to slide her foot up and down the outside of Clayton's right calf. Leaning back with his eyes closed, he pretended not to notice. She put her foot on his knee and then slowly, ever so slowly, slid it in between his thighs. Instantly his thighs shut around her foot. She tried to pull it free. He reached for her foot taking it by the ankle, and firmly placed her heel against his erection. With his hands as a gentle guide, she rubbed her foot softly up and down the length of his cock.

"Stand up," he quietly commanded. "Get in the center of the tub, and spread your legs."

She did as he directed. He reached up, cupped her buttocks and gently began to play with them. He slapped, stroked and fondled them. He spread her cheeks and pushed them together again. He stood up just enough to reach her mouth in a long, passionate kiss. Then he moved his attention to her breasts, licking and sucking first one then the other. He trailed his mouth slowly down towards her navel. Although her navel was under water, he covered it with his mouth. He came up for air and then ducked his head under the warm water again. He found her pussy with his mouth and tongued it, then gently blew all his air into it, tickling her. She smiled softly. He surfaced, took a deep breath and repeated the procedure.

Clayton sat back on his seat and pulled Sherry down onto his erect cock. He leaned back and she leaned with him. She kissed him passionately, her hands holding onto the side of the tub. He slid his hands from her waist to her buttocks. Together they began to rock up and down with a slow, steady rhythm that built to a faster and faster pace. When they were both about to reach their crest they paused, savoring the sensations and then began again, moving slowly and once again gradually building up speed. Time after time they almost reached the peak and then paused, until finally they came with orgasms that left them both breathless.

When they had recovered enough to stand, they got out of the hot tub, turned it off and went into the house. They took a short shower together just to wash off the chlorine, and went in to eat the beef stew Sherry had made for dinner. They ate and sat quietly talking over the day's events. They washed the few dishes together and put away the leftovers before they went up to bed. Once they were in bed they made love again, but this time with more of a quiet tenderness and a little less frenzy. Finally, when they were just about to drift off to sleep, the baby started to cry.

"It could have been worse." Sherry sat up, and watched Clay as he went to get the baby. "She could have cried while we were still in the tub."

"She could have cried while I was still in you," Clayton quipped, as he paused briefly at the door. He wiggled his eyebrows and shot her a lecherous leer.

After a few minutes he brought the baby to Sherry and sat on the bed naked, watching her nurse. The mother and daughter looked so angelic together that he felt his heart would burst with love. When the baby, Christina, was finished nursing and had drifted off to sleep, he gently put her back in her crib. By the time he returned to bed Sherry was asleep. He cuddled up close to her and fell asleep himself.

Clay woke up earlier than Sherry. He didn't wake her; he just lay there next to her and thought about their lives together and how they had met. He couldn't believe how far they had come since the day they first met.

They had been club members and lovers long before James and Suzanne had joined the club. In fact, they had been club members for over three years and lovers for five.

They had met when they both auditioned for a musical that the Community Theatre was putting on. As it happened, they got the leads. The musical was *Kiss Me Kate*.

They were both doing well in the play except for the spanking scene. It just never seemed real, or even right. The director asked them to practice the scene by themselves to try to "liven it up."

Finally Clayton had an outlandish idea. He asked Sherry to come over to his house for dinner and a private rehearsal, and to wear the full skirts she wore during the rehearsals. He hoped Sherry wouldn't get too mad since she seemed like a nice girl. Clayton set up a video camera and they worked on the scene. The first time through they did it the same way they had been, but tried to put more feeling into it.

Watching it, Sherry said, sounding disgusted, "It just doesn't work, it lacks something."

"Let's try it again, I have an idea," Clay said with a nervous grin. "It may help."

They did the scene again, only this time he didn't give her a fake spanking over her thick, lacy petticoats. Instead, he flipped the petticoats up onto her back and pulled down her underwear. Then he gave her a very real and very painful spanking on her bare butt.

Sherry was shocked. She had never even dreamed of being spanked as an adult by a man she hardly knew. She struggled and yelled out loud. When he let her up, she slapped Clayton hard, right across the mouth. Finally when she calmed down, they watched the videotape together. They both had to admit it: the performance was better, it had the real quality the director wanted.

"I don't care how good it is," Sherry told Clay firmly, "there is no way you're going to get me to go bare butt on stage."

"But it is better if I really spank you, isn't it?" Clay asked reasonably.

"Yes, I guess," Sherry admitted, mumbling.

"And was it really too painful?" he asked, probing.

"No, it was more of a shock than anything," she admitted. "There was some real pain but it faded quickly."

"Could you take it? On stage, I mean?" he pushed.

"Sure, for eight performances, I guess I could," she admitted weakly.

"Then get a pair of lacy pantaloons, and I can spank you over them." Clayton grinned. "I won't spank you as hard or the same way each time, so there will still be some surprise and some freshness in each performance. How does that sound?"

"Like you should play Kate." She raised her eyebrows at him.

"Sorry, but I don't fit in the costume." He grinned at her. "Even if I did, you look much better in it than I do."

"I think we should leave the slap in," she teased.

"Surprise me." He winked at her.

He stood up and walked her to the door. He stopped at the door, enfolding her in a warm hug and kissed her for the first time ever, except on stage. The kiss quickly grew. After that first kiss, she didn't go home.

The play was a great success. Clayton spanked Sherry nightly on stage, usually not extremely hard but for opening night he was relentless. On closing night Sherry had a surprise for him.

In spite of her nervousness, on closing night she left off her lacy pantaloons. Clay didn't find out until he flipped up her petticoats in the scene. In spite of the surprise, he gave her a very hard spanking right there on stage, directly on her bare butt! Neither one of them ever really admitted even to themselves what was going on though, until they caught themselves practicing the spanking scene one night about a month after the run of the musical was ended.

They sat down and had a long frank talk about how much Clay enjoyed spanking her. For the first time she tried returning the favor, spanking him. They had to admit they enjoyed spanking each other, although she preferred to be the bottom to his top. A lucky thing, since he was more of a top.

Soon after that they went looking quietly for people with similar interests, to find out about things like books and movies, props, and whether there were any social organizations they could join. Clayton had to be careful because at the time he was a trial lawyer with a certain reputation to uphold, but they still managed to find several clubs in nearby towns.

The problem was that most of the clubs they found at first either had more gay members than straight, or featured group or promiscuous sex. They had no objection to the gay members; they only wanted to be among people with interests closer to theirs. They strongly objected, however, to the clubs that featured group sex and promiscuity. The next few clubs they found were more BDSM, and not spanking groups. Although BDSM could encompass spanking, it had more rules and protocols than they were looking for; it just wasn't quite right for them.

The Paddle Club, which they found shortly after they had begun to live together, had been a godsend at first, but soon they began to get bored with the club. The club members were nice and the club suited their personalities, but the club itself was getting stagnate. They had been on the verge of quitting the club for that very reason when James came along.

He revitalized the club, making it more fun and giving it a younger, fresher outlook. Suzanne's arrival had completed the rejuvenation process. Now the club parties were fun, social and spirited. Clay smiled as he thought of some of the things they had done in the club. He began to laugh out loud as he thought of the woman who had visited one regular party, the concerned citizen.

By now Sherry was awake. "What's so funny?" she asked, sliding her hand up his leg.

"I was remembering that woman, what was her name? The concerned citizen."

"Carol?" Sherry smiled at the memory of how they had ambushed the snoop. "What about her?"

"I wonder what she would have said if she had known that I was the City Attorney!"

"It would have been a sight to see if she had shown up in your office after the party to try to get the club shut down," Sherry laughed.

Chapter Eighteen

Just Horsing Around

The day after the spanking fair was a Sunday. Toni and Mario spent the day relaxing and resting. They were both recovering from the Trade Show, their first experience with the club. They were both horse lovers but for some reason the very thought of riding didn't appeal very much to either of them on that particular Sunday. There was one small problem, something a bit uncomfortable about the thought of tender butts coming into contact with hard, leather saddles.

They went out to the boarding stables and exercised the horses without riding them. For once, the busy ranch was almost empty. It was especially rare for it to be so quiet on a beautiful, summer weekend, but there was a big horse show at an arena about ten miles away.

They exercised the horses from the ground in the small round bull pen. First they worked Toni's small, quick bay gelding. Mario had him trot around the bullpen until he was warmed up, reversing him several times. Then he had the gelding lope until the horse was well exercised and beginning to sweat. Then Mario took the horse over to the washing rack, tied him there and washed him. He put the horse on the hot walker while Toni worked Mario's tall, sorrel gelding. Then he washed the copper colored horse. In a short time, both horses were walking quietly but reluctantly on the walker. They both had the equine equivalent of being highly put upon on their faces, ears halfway back and lower lips protruding.

The hot walker, run by a small electric motor, has a center pole and four long arms that extended from the pole like spokes on a wheel. The arms have snaps and chains that hang down so that a horse's halter can be snapped to it. The pole rotates and pulls the horses in a slow walk around in a small circle. It keeps the horse moving long enough to dry off or cool down without getting chilled too quickly.

Toni and Mario sat on the ground under a tree and watched the horses plod around the circle. They had a small picnic basket and a blanket which they spread out, and stretched out under the shady tree. Since no one was around, they kissed and cuddled. They dug into the picnic basket and ate their cold chicken and potato salad, and talked about the club. Toni told Mario some of the things she had learned about the club following the call she had that morning from Suzanne.

"She said that if we wanted to join, she would sponsor us. Suzanne told me that most of the members join as couples, and most of them have long-term committed relationships. The standard rule is that spankings and whippings are public, while any sexual contact is private between the two people involved," Toni explained. "This is not a swinger's club. Members who make too many advances to another member's partner are blackballed and thrown out."

"That's good to know." Mario leaned over and kissed her soundly, before reaching into the hamper for a piece of chocolate cake. "I don't want to share you."

"She also said that most of the couples, regardless of how it seems, don't just spank each other all day and night. They usually save that for the monthly parties and special events. Most of them seem to have fairly normal home lives." Toni grinned. "But I think sometimes the members do it in private too. It's really meant to be more of a role playing thing than real S & M."

"Then role playing can really hurt, can't it?" he managed, remembering the fair between bites of cake. "And it can cause real bruises too. What else did she say?"

"She told me about the clubhouse. The building where they hold the club parties was inherited by one of the members, who happens to be fairly rich, along with the grounds around it. It's actually still his property, but the club has full use of it in return for keeping it up and paying the expenses. They also lease it out for special occasions when they don't have anything scheduled. By the way, the club is incorporated as a non-profit organization, and all its proceeds after upkeep on the building go to support two charities. You'll never guess which two," she challenged.

"Let's see. How about a mental health clinic, and the blood bank?" he guessed.

"The mental health guess is not far off. They support a child abuse prevention hotline and a shelter for battered women." She grabbed an apple and bit into it.

"Both worthy causes, and appropriate for a club that some people might think encourages violence against women, and even kids," Mario replied thoughtfully.

"But that's the point, they work hard to keep anyone who's really turned on by violence out. They want members who enjoy acting out things, without permanently hurting each other. And everything has to be agreeable to everyone involved. Also, according to Suzanne there is a rather painful initiation." Toni smiled, "I can't figure out how painful it can be when they're supposed to be so strong against really hurting someone. Suzanne said something about stinging and maybe a few bruises but no real injuries."

"I suppose she means that it won't be any worse than yesterday," Mario said. "And as hard as it hurt yesterday, there's only a trace of tenderness left today."

"Anyway, the next initiation is scheduled to be held in about three weeks. If we want to join, we can decide any time before that." She finished the apple and lay back on the ground.

"We'll decide later." Mario was too relaxed and drowsy to think. "I should go put the horses up before they walk their legs off."

"I'll do it, sweetheart, you take a nap." She kissed him, got up, and went over to turn off the hot walker.

Both horses nickered eagerly to be taken off the boring equipment. The minute she turned the machine off so that it stopped pulling on them, they both, in a symbol of equine practicality, stood still and peed, not even moving as she unsnapped one of them from the end of the chains. Avoiding the strong smelling muddy spot, she led the first horse out of the walker and looped his rope over a fence rail, then unfastened the other.

She swung up onto her gelding and rode him back to their stalls with the other horse's lead rope in her right hand. The horses were both restless from being on the walker and they wanted to act up but Toni kept them under tight control. She put the horses in their stalls at just about the same time the hay truck was coming by with their evening hay. She gave them each an apple, a scoop of grain and some vitamins. Then locked up her tack boxes, made sure the stall doors were securely fastened and went back to Mario.

He was sound asleep. It was too much of a temptation to resist; she reached into the ice cooler and got a handful of ice cubes. She put them on his stomach where his shirt had ridden up. He slept for a second more, and then awoke with a loud yell.

"Woman, you're in trouble!" He rolled her over and gave her a few sharp, playful swats on the seat of her faded blue jeans. "I'm taking you home right now."

He stood up and reached down to pick her up. He threw her over his shoulder and swatted her on her butt.

"Good idea, as the ranch hands are starting to talk," Toni teased him, her head hanging down.

Mario spoke to Miguel, the nearest hand, in Spanish and he answered with a wide grin. Both men looked at Toni's butt. The hired hand spoke again, still smiling a wide, hearty smile. Mario nodded and waved, patting her fanny.

"Si, amigo, gracias," he told the man. "Por favor?" He gestured at the remains of the picnic.

The obliging ranch hand picked up the lunch and folded the blanket. The man followed Mario to his truck and put his things in the back for him.

"Adiós, Miguel, muy gracias." Mario said.

Miguel waved and grinned before walking away.

"What was that all about?" Toni asked as Mario set her in the cab of the truck.

"Miguel saw you put the ice on me and watched me swat your butt. He suggested that I take you home and beat you soundly for disturbing my nap and then fuck you like crazy," Mario grinned. "I thanked him for the suggestion."

"Are you going to follow it?" Toni asked quietly.

"That's none of your business," he replied, raising his eyebrows. "So don't even ask."

"None of my business, my butt!" she said, her voice raised. "What do you mean none of my business?"

"Precisely," Mario said, "it is my business and my butt." He patted her ass in a proprietary manner.

"Ah, ha. Muy macho hombre," she teased him, using almost all her Spanish. "You think."

When they got home they took a long shower, washing the dirt and smell of horses off their bodies. They spent a long time soaping each other and gently arousing one another in the warm, steamy shower. They toweled each other dry and Mario used the blow dryer to dry her hair.

They pulled down the spread and got into bed. Mario pulled her gently into his arms and then suddenly wrestled her into a position so that she was lying across his lap, with her head hanging off the side of the bed. Her shoulder length, curly brown hair was hanging down towards the floor.

Mario spanked her slowly and not very hard, with Toni laughing and struggling all the while. After about a dozen slaps he began to spank her more harshly. The slaps were stinging but not painful. Toni was still laughing and trying to get upright.

"Say that you're sorry," Mario ordered, still spanking her.

"Sorry for what?" Toni asked. "I was a perfect lady."

"Sorry for the ice and waking me out of a peaceful Sunday afternoon nap," he replied, spanking her harder now, each slap turning her full round butt red. "Sorry for being such a brat."

"Okay, okay. Alright, already," she laughed. "Sorry, uncle, whatever you want."

"Whatever I want?" Mario asked slowly. He paused, his hand

still raised in the air.

"Yes." She was laughing.

He gave her one last hard spank before he pulled her up onto the bed, rolled her over and climbed on top of her. Slowly using his hands and mouth, he worked his way down her voluptuous body; he kissed and nibbled on every square inch of it except for the apex of her thighs. He asked her to roll over and started at her feet, slowly working his way up sucking, licking and kissing slowly up her backside. On this side he skipped her red and slightly tender buttocks.

When he got to the nape of her neck he came back down, this time spending a long time gently kissing and biting her butt. He bathed her warm, pink cheeks with his wet tongue. His long hair slid over her skin as he worked. His tongue even found the crack of her ass. He rolled her over and lifted her legs up onto his shoulders, making love to her with tongue and mouth.

When she had climaxed, he held her gently. He let her come down from her orgasm before bring his mouth to hers again.

Sitting astride her, he asked her to push her breasts together. He slid his cock in and out of her cleavage several times before he moved farther up her body until he was kneeling with his large erect cock near her mouth.

"You said anything." His voice was quiet.

"I meant it too," Toni smiled.

She took him into her mouth, using her tongue and lips to bring him to a shuttering climax. They lay there quietly for several minutes, resting and cuddling each other. Soon it started again. Cuddling became kissing. Kissing soon turned from affection to foreplay. Before long he was erect and she was wet, again.

Rolling over on top of her, he slid his cock into her gently and began to make love to her with all the passion and tenderness she could ever imagine. This time when they stopped they were so drenched with sweat that they had to put on the air conditioner to cool off. Pretty soon Mario reached down and pulled up a sheet to prevent them from cooling off too fast.

"So, are we going to join the club, or not?" Toni asked.

"We're in." He kissed her all over her face, finally honing in on her swollen mouth. "If you can stand to see all those other women getting spanked by me, and spanking me in return."

"Or other men?" she teased, gasping as he lowered his mouth to her breast, suckling gently at it and teasing the nipple with his tongue. "Mario? Honestly, I don't care who you spank or who spanks you, as long as I'm the only one who makes love to you. Deal?"

"Deal," he agreed. Then Mario asked, "Shall we seal it with a kiss?"

"We'll start with a kiss," she reached up for him, "and see what comes up."

Chapter Nineteen

New Victims, Er, New Members

Once again Suzanne was nervous as she dressed for the Paddle Club initiation. This time because it was her turn to be acting as the club's hostess for the evening. She was picked to be this night's hostess because her friend Toni and Toni's longtime companion, Mario, were two of the four people being initiated. The other couple, Sarah and Mac, were complete strangers to Suzanne however she had talked to both of them on the phone and they seemed to be a very nice, loving couple.

It was kind of a mystery, however, just who originally suggested that they apply to the club for membership. Suzanne went on her instincts and offered to sponsor their membership herself.

The most interesting thing about this couple, Suzanne found out, was that Mac used to advertise in the singles' newspapers as a dom and get paid by women, and even a few men, for spanking, beating and whipping them. In fact, Sarah was a paying customer when she met Mac. The couple was very up front about it because they didn't want to hide anything. Mac was unashamed and completely open about his past business.

Suzanne was reviewing all the arrangements she was responsible for during the initiation. She went over her mental list of things to do, checking off each completed item in her mind. She mentally reviewed everything she knew about the people involved. She was just pulling her formal, violet beaded gown over her head when she heard James come into the bedroom.

"Are you about ready, my dear?" He kissed her neck.

"Yes, I am, As soon as I get this bracelet fastened. Can you do it?" She held out her hand and the troublesome bracelet.

While he was fighting the tiny clasp, she asked, "Is the sitter

139

downstairs?"

"She sure is." He paused before saying in a serious tone, "I'll stay here with the twins for a minute while you go downstairs and talk to her."

"What's up?" Suzanne instantly noticed his concern.

"I think her boyfriend beat her up. Really beat her up," James told her. "And I didn't want to be the one to try to talk to her about it."

"Oh my God!" Suzanne hurried down the stairs.

When she saw Janie the very first thing she noticed was that the girl had been crying. Her fair skin was puffy, damp and blotchy. Then Janie turned her head and Suzanne saw the large, ugly bruise on her jaw, and noticed several small, blotchy bruises on her arms. Her green eyes were red-rimmed and swollen. She looked bedraggled, with her long brown hair hanging unkempt and limp.

"Did Freddie do this to you?" Suzanne asked gently, softly stroking the bruise on her jaw.

"Yes he did, but he didn't mean to hit me," Janie replied, defending Freddie. "It was an accident."

"Janie, listen to me. There is no way to give someone a sock in the jaw accidentally. And, this is not the first time! Face it Janie, he's an abusive creep!" Suzanne said firmly.

"I deserved it!" Janie sniffed. "I'm always doing something that makes him mad."

"No, you didn't deserve it, no matter what, even if you did something to make him mad." She lifted the girl's chin, gently looking her straight in the eye. "He should never hit you. No real man beats a woman."

"But I thought you'd understand. You and James," she blushed, but continued, "I mean, um-"

"I don't know what you think you know about James and me, but I'll tell you the truth," Suzanne said gently and calmly. "It's something I try to keep very private and personal, just so nobody will misunderstand. But maybe now it will help you to see clearly what's happening to you."

"James and I play sex games that involve spankings. Sometimes he spanks me and sometimes I spank him. Yes, I really do." She had to smile at the shock on Janie's face. "But we only do it as a game, for fun. He has never ever hurt me and he has never, and I mean never, hit me in anger or frustration, not ever. He doesn't put bruises on me, and he certainly doesn't make me feel worthless or inadequate. In fact, he makes me feel as if I'm the most beautiful, special woman in the world."

"Gee, I wonder why," Janie said dryly. "Face it, you are so beautiful, not to mention smart and funny, it's enough to give us normal girls a complex."

"Thanks Janie. I just try to do my best with what I've got, like anyone else. Trust me; I have my faults, too." Suzanne promised herself to help the girl gain some self-esteem. "But back to what I was saying. For us, these spankings are a part of our sexuality, acting out a role, like in a play, and they are not abuse. Neither one of us has ever even spanked the girls. Of course they are still babies, but neither one of us believes in spanking as a punishment for children anyway. The reason I can play these games is that I know, as sure as I'm sitting here, James will never do to me what Freddie did to you. Please, listen to me. You don't have to take it, not for a minute, not even for a second. You deserve to be treated much better than that. Break up with him now, tonight. Okay?"

"Thanks for telling me that; I know it's very hard to tell someone about something so private. Let me think tonight while I'm here. Maybe I've been wrong." Janie gave her a faint smile.

"Sweetie, James and I will help you in any way we can. While you're here tonight why don't you soak in the bathtub and relax. Or go for a swim. Then take a nice nap. Believe me, the twins will let you know if they need you. Just be very careful if you go into the pool alone." Suzanne hugged the girl, then she called out, "James, let's go. We can't be late!"

Once they were in the car, James asked her, "How's Janie doing?"

"I talked to her but I don't know for sure if she really heard me

141

and understood what I had to say. It's got to be her choice to leave the relationship. She knew something about us though. About our spankings."

"Did that make it harder for you to advise her to leave Freddie?" James asked.

"I don't think so. I tried to use it to show the difference between you and that creep, the difference between what we do and what he does. It may even have helped," Suzanne calmly replied.

"No wonder she was looking at me so strangely when we left," James laughed softly.

"She loved it when I got to the part where I told her that sometimes I spank you." Suzanne smiled slyly.

"You didn't." He flushed a little.

"I sure did, I told her the whole truth." She grinned. "She doesn't need lies right now."

"I'll get you for that," he joked.

"Promises, promises, always promises." She stuck her tongue out at him playfully, then hugged him. "And no action."

They stopped to pick up Sherry and Clayton. James went to the door to get them.

"Hi. I hope we're not late," he said as he greeted the other couple.

"Nope, you're right on time. Our sitter just got here." Sherry smiled, "It still seems funny to realize that we're all old respectable married couples now, with kids and everything."

"Yeah, but we're still kinky as hell," Clay added, laughing. "Thank God."

The group of friends made their way to the car and got in. Clayton and Sherry greeted Suzanne. Sherry looked fabulous in a gown that matched both her coloring and her name. It was the exact color of a fine bottle of Sherry. Clayton was dressed in his tuxedo and looked like a model for the groom on top of a wedding cake.

Sherry told Suzanne, "We were just talking about how we all have our own families now."

"I still think it's strange that your daughter was born almost nine months to the day after the *Amazing Maze*," James told the other pair.

"No, it's not so strange," Suzanne said. "I'm sorry but somehow I forgot to stock that particular bedroom with condoms."

"Suzanne, you never forgot anything like that in your life," Sherry told her. "Admit it, you set us up."

"Well, I was feeling left out and a little mischievous because all I could do was be the voice," Suzanne admitted. "I was pregnant with the twins. It seemed like a good idea at the time."

"As it turns out, it was the best idea of your life," Clayton admitted. "But I still owe you for all the extra torture you put me through. I never could figure out your uncanny sense of timing. Sherry managed to have orgasms at some of the stops but you stopped me too soon every damned time."

"Poor baby. This sure seems to be my night for threats," Suzanne complained. "First James and now you."

"Why did James threaten you?" Sherry asked.

"She told the babysitter that she likes to spank me," James answered for her, deadpanned.

"Suzanne! You didn't!" Even Sherry was shocked. "No wonder James is threatening to beat your body."

James pulled into the large club hall, parked and they all got out. They saw Toni and Mario getting out of the limo. All six friends went into the hall together, talking.

Suzanne found Jerry, the limo driver, just getting ready to go pick up the second couple. She checked the address with him and made sure the limo had all the necessary supplies. Champagne, lotion and condoms, everything a sore but also aroused couple might need after being whipped in an initiation ceremony.

"We'll send the second couple home in a second limo; it will be here at eleven. Before you take your couple home, would you check it for supplies? A strange limo driver might not know about the need for lotion," she asked.

"Because of the sore butts?" Jerry laughed, remembering other initiations. "I'll take care of everything, Lass."

"Thanks Jerry." Suzanne kissed him on the check. As she turned away he swatted her sharply on the butt.

"No fair," she complained. "Do it right."

She turned her back to him and pulled up her long dress. He gave her a smart spanking; only about a dozen slaps. The last two or three were the only ones that stung, and then he stopped.

"That's all for now, you greedy girl. I don't want to be late picking up this couple." Jerry smiled at her.

"Okay, Jerry, get going." She smiled at him, "And thanks."

"Anytime, sweet cheeks." Jerry grinned back.

Chapter Twenty

Another Painful Initiation

When Suzanne got to the main room she found James, Clay, Sherry, Toni, Mario and Edna all embroiled in a deep discussion. As she joined the group some of the other members walked over. Some of them recognized Toni and Mario from the trade show, but Suzanne made the formal introductions.

James quickly turned the discussion back to business. "The most important thing now is to plan another gala. Our new goal is to have a charity fundraiser every three months. We have the next *Maze* again in a month and the Trade Show in another six months, and those are good ideas. We can update them every year to keep them fresh, and still hold them annually. But we need some more ideas, any suggestions?"

An older, gray haired man suggested, "How about having a Harem Night?"

Suzanne replied, "I don't really think that's such a good idea. According to everything I've ever heard about a harem, only the women ever get whipped. Besides, all the men except the owner of the harem have to be castrated to prevent them from having sex with the master's women." She winked at the older man.

The man said formally, with a straight face, "I hereby withdraw the suggestion." Several club members laughed.

Someone else made a suggestion. "We could have a slave auction, though."

"That would have to be handled very carefully or it could get out of hand. We don't want anyone who might go too far," James said. "But it's certainly worth discussing."

The small group discussed the idea briefly, and two of the members agreed to draw up an initial plan for the event so that it could be discussed online, then brought up at a general meeting and voted on.

James looked around the table. "Any other ideas?" he asked.

"I didn't want to bring this up until I had more details, but what if we chartered a cruise ship?" Clay suggested. "I think I know how to get a deal on one."

"You mean for club members only?" James asked.

"Yes, or sharing with another group, if they would be agreeable," Clay said. "Like I said, I'm still researching it. I'll know more by the next party."

"Anyone else?" James asked.

"I don't know how to make this fit in with our other club activities," one woman said shyly, "but how about a casino night?"

"That could be a good idea." James said. "We could even set it up so that the general public could be invited. It would give them a chance to enter the 'Lion's den' and see what we're really like. We'll have to think about it. How about a carnival? I have some ideas. I think we should hold a real carnival during the day, one that our kids and the general public can go to, and then kink it up for the adults at night."

"That sounds pretty good. What kind of kink?" Jerry asked.

"Maybe someone could be on the merry-go-round to whip the rider's asses when they go by. The games can use swats as prizes. We'll just have to be very creative. Like the thing where you try to ring a bell and a dunk tank. And of course a kissing or swatting booth."

"We'll have to discuss it in a lot more detail later," Suzanne interrupted. "Here comes the other new couple."

The couple, Sarah and Mac, were greeted by Suzanne. She brought them over to the group and introduced them. Sarah was a redhead, with short bouncy curls and big green eyes. She was slender but well curved, with a firm rounded ass. Even with her fiery hair and flashing green eyes she seemed shy, almost meek. It was definitely a false impression. She looked beautiful in an emerald green, silk formal gown. Mac turned out to be drop dead gorgeous; he had dark wavy hair with bright blue eyes and a very muscular build. He had a chiseled, handsome face with a great smile and a warm friendly voice. He looked like the only reason tuxedos were ever invented.

"Wow!" Edna whispered. "Someone who looks even better in a tuxedo than Clay."

"Hard to believe isn't it?" Suzanne whispered back.

Suzanne finished her drink and led the couples to their chairs on the platform. As tradition had it, the initiation began with the old members lining up to be whipped by the prospective new members. Of the new members, Mario gave everyone in front of him a good hard whipping, but Mac had a real talent for knowing just how hard to make the blows. He also knew just where on each person to land the blows and when to ease up to almost gentle taps, and when to build up the force of the blows, even when to quit. Out of all the people in the room, only Sarah and Suzanne knew that his notable expertise came from a great deal of professional experience.

Sarah also had a small amount of professional experience and she did a good job with the people who waited in line for her to whip them. Toni turned out to be the most tentative when it came to whipping people, and even she did a fairly decent job; much better than the job Suzanne did at her own initiation.

After a short break Sarah was strapped down and whipped by the membership. She bore it very well; in fact she really even seemed to enjoy it. She was really a natural bottom. Mac gave her the final six swats with the heavy paddle, right on top of the welts caused by the birch rods. He was very harsh with her, laying on the swats as slow and as hard as he could.

Mac was birched next. He actually didn't enjoy it very much; his specialty was to give rather than to receive. He was good-natured and cooperative; however only his lusty yells gave him away. Sarah returned the favor and gave him the six final swats with the paddle as hard as she could.

Next it was Toni's turn to be birched. She was very apprehensive remembering how hard she had been birched at the fair. She let herself be strapped down without making any protest, however. Mario gently stroked her hair and kissed her neck as he helped Suzanne fasten the straps. She was birched first by Suzanne, then by club members who were lined up behind her. When she started to protest the birching stopped immediately, and Mario gave her the final six blows with the paddle. Although he put some muscle into it, he was not especially harsh.

His turn was next and he seemed to enjoy the process almost to the end of the birching. The last few slashes of the birch, however, seemed to really hurt him. Toni paddled him solidly but not very harshly.

There was a discussion among the membership, and the four new members were admitted to the club. There was no question really; they were all nice, fun and energetic people. The old members gathered around to welcome the new members into the club and get to know them. All four of the new members were not allowed to dress, and they were all a little self-conscious with their nudity in the crowd, but the regular members seemed not to notice. Toni finally spotted Jerry and Edna, whom she remembered from the fair. She went over and hugged them, then introduced them to Mario.

"These are the two people who arranged for me to surprise you in the middle of the fair," Toni explained to Mario, then she turned to Jerry. "I didn't see you earlier."

"I drove you here but I stayed behind the dark glass. I'm the club chauffeur," he said, by way of explanation. "I had to go pick up the other couple so I couldn't stop to talk. You're both wearing some of my welts on your sore behinds though," he said with a wide grin.

"Mine too," Edna added.

"Gee, thanks a lot," Mario said, sounding as if he was not really quite sure that he meant it.

Jerry and Edna both laughed. They waited while the couple said their good-byes to everyone and walked with them to the limo. They stood by the limo and chatted with Toni and Mario while they got dressed. With Edna beside him, Jerry drove the young couple home. In the back seat of the limo the supply of soothing lotion, champagne and condoms were all diminished by the time Jerry pulled up in front of their house.

Sarah and Mac had their clothes brought to them in the room before they went out to the limo waiting in the garage because their driver was not a club member. He was hired as an extra driver for this one night. Sarah and Mac said their farewells and got into the limo.

As soon as all the new members were gone everyone started to relax. Clayton met James' eyes and nodded at him across the room. They both made their way casually around the room, sneaking up on Suzanne. Each one took her by one of her elbows. They led her over to the bench and strapped her down.

"We both have a score to settle with you, remember Suzanne?" James prodded her. "Telling family secrets is my gripe, and Clay seems to think you were deliberately unfair to him when he was in the maze."

"I was, I admit it," she said, sighing dramatically. "Go ahead and punish me."

"Oh we will, hot cheeks, we will." James brought the paddle down on her butt with a loud crack.

They took turns paddling Suzanne until she started to yell then they stopped, leaving her tied up. The two men walked around the room, chatting and socializing, with Suzanne still in position on the bench. The only people who came over to visit with her picked up the paddle and used it on her, sometimes just a token swat, and sometimes very harshly. Both couples stayed later than usual at the party.

Finally, when everyone else had gone home, Clay and James came back to finish dealing with Suzanne. They gagged her and picked up the paddle, beating her again. Harshly, but not really causing any injury to her, just fast, loud, stinging blows.

When they let her up, she stood on unsteady feet and apologized for her actions. Her apology was ruined by the sly grin on her face.

"I don't think she's really very penitent, do you, James?" Clay asked cynically.

"No. But I'll forgive her anyway." James grinned at his wife. "What about you, Clay?"

"Yeah, I'll forgive her this time." Clay grinned. "She's usually a pretty damn good woman. Besides, I don't have time to paddle her any more because I have more important things to do. I have to take my wife home and make love to her, right now."

"I guess I could use some time alone with my wife too." James gave Suzanne a look that caused her blood to race.

Chapter Twenty-one

The Photo Shoot

Sarah and Mac drank some of the icy champagne and made stormy love in the limo during their long ride home. They said their good nights to the driver and took the open bottle into the house and finished it in bed before they made love again.

Afterwards, they cuddled together in bed and talked over the Paddle Club and people they had just met. It seemed the club might even be good for Mac's business. Mac told Sarah that their advertising firm was doing the new ad campaign for James' law firm. He had also made some other contacts. Their advertising firm was still new; they started it shortly after they had become lovers.

"This club could turn out to be a gold mine for our business, as well as our social lives," Mac said enthusiastically.

"I'm just glad we met so many nice people with similar tastes to ours," Sarah said with a smile. "Any advertising business we get from club members is a bonus."

"I really enjoyed talking with Suzanne and James, and Jerry and Edna. And I liked Sherry and Clayton, a lot." Mac kissed her.

"I thought Clay was the most like you of all the people there, at least in the way he whipped someone, I mean. He was very stern with a no-nonsense approach and a harsh stroke," Sarah told him. "But James has a warm fun-loving grin that reminds me of yours."

After meeting Sarah, Mac's enthusiasm for earning his money by giving good hard whippings to people who answered his ad in the underground newspapers had quickly faded. Before long, he dropped the ads altogether. He had also given up his kinky phone lines. He was getting positively respectable! He had walked a balancing act for years, never quite acting as a gigolo or

151

a male prostitute, but using his hands to give people, primarily women, pleasure by spanking, teasing and even whipping them.

The change was Sarah's fault, or her credit, depending on how he looked at it. She had shown him that being sexual and adventurous didn't mean he had to live without any personal values. A truly committed relationship didn't have to stop him from having fun. He was sure that the club would give them the outlet for their games and fantasies with friends, without the impersonal quality that comes from being paid to please someone else.

Mac was still hungry and he wanted more champagne. They got out of bed and went into the kitchen, naked. Mac pulled some leftover roast beef out of the refrigerator. He sliced the meat thinly, and they made cold roast beef and cheese sandwiches. Sarah got out some grapes and they opened another bottle of champagne and poured it into tall fluted goblets. They sat at the kitchen table and ate, laughing and talking about the evening.

Mac made a smart aleck remark about how beautiful some of the women were; teasing Sarah and trying to provoke her jealousy. He failed.

She threw a grape at him, and said with wide-eyed enthusiasm, "Did you see James? What a hunk, and that curly blonde hair made me want to run my fingers through it. Clayton is great looking too. He has that darkly handsome and stern look, as if he can see right into your soul. He made me shiver."

Mac pretended to be provoked, rising from his chair and lunging at her. He wrestled her down to the clean, hard, linoleum floor. He straddled her using his legs to hold her arms down and pinning her hands with his, holding them over her head. She was immobilized, except for a small range of motion by lifting her head.

"So what are you going to do now, my love?" he asked as she struggled to get free.

"There's not much I can do, only this." She raised her head enough to take his cock into her mouth.

Rolling over and taking her with him, he shifted his hold on her hands until he was holding them both in one of his hands. He reached up for the bottle of champagne and poured it on her body. He spent several long minutes licking it off her, paying special attention to all her little cracks and crevices.

Then he poured the rest of the champagne on his body. She moved her mouth from his cock long enough to take a mouthful of the champagne from his navel before it all spilled on the floor. She took his cock into her mouth again, the cold champagne causing him to have shivers up and down his spine. She sucked him until he was in such a fever that he became a wild man. Just before he came he rolled her over and clasped her hands above her head. He plunged into her with an almost savage frenzy and fucked her wildly until he came. He didn't withdraw or release her hands to let her move until he felt the shivers stop running through her body.

As they lay on the floor together she raised herself up on one elbow and said sweetly, "This time you have to mop the kitchen floor."

"It's worth it. At least this way we keep the kitchen floor clean," he laughed and kissed her. "How's your backside?"

"Tender, but not bad." She asked him, "Did I get any welts?"

"Some. Shall we take pictures?" Mac asked.

"Sure, for our album," she cuddled him, "and we can look at some of our oldies but goodies while they develop."

The night they met, when she went to him and paid for a spanking, he had taken pictures of her. First he had spanked her and used a riding crop to whip her, and then by unspoken but mutual consent, they went past the original agreement. Way past the original agreement. For the first time ever with a paid client he used his hands, his mouth and his cock on her in every sexual way he knew how.

He gave her plenty of chances to refuse at each new sensation, but he kept her agreeing to anything he wanted to do by saying in a laughing voice, "Trust me."

She was with him every step of the way. She gave her consent and fully participated as much as she possibly could, although for most of that long, memorable night he had her tied up.

He had taken pictures of her after beating her savagely with the riding crop; she was tied up and bent over the bed with her feet tied to the bedposts. Her hands were tied to the bedposts at the head of the bed. Her buttocks were red and covered with welts.

After the pictures he had pulled out a birch rod and told her to ask him for a severe birching. For some reason, unbeknownst to even herself, she did just that. On that night she did everything just as he asked. Using a tripod and a remote button he took a few pictures of the birch actually hitting her, and a few after he finished with the birch rod.

He untied her, had her kiss and put away the birch, and then retied her. Then he sodomized her; he was gentle and patient entering her. He even managed to snap a few pictures of his cock in her anus before throwing the camera aside and beginning to pump her, building into a frantic climax.

Her trust in him was rewarded a hundred times over by the fantastic sex and the tender, gentle side of his nature. He was caring and loving.

That night he refunded the money she'd paid him and gave her the roll of film. He wanted her to know that what had happened between them was real, not part of any sex-for-hire thing. He gave her the film so she would know that the pictures he took were for her enjoyment, and not for any future use in blackmail or harassment. He still shook his head at himself when he remembered returning the money, as it was a definite first for him. That's what happens when you fall in love.

For a short time they both worked together getting paid to chastise people, but it seemed to be less rewarding to both of them than it was worth. Shortly after moving in together they opened an ad agency, and after a few months, they decided to get married.

Mac ran the mop over the floor, quickly getting up any traces of champagne. He went into the studio and found Sarah setting up the camera and lights. He looked at her butt, noticing that the redness was already fading and the welts disappearing.

"Do you want a touch up to bring out the color?" he asked her. He took a test shot with the instant camera.

She watched it develop and studied the results. "Yeah, I think so."

Mac pulled out a birch rod. She bent over, holding the seat of a chair. He birched her, using just enough force to bring up the color on her butt. He gave her two or three hard slashes with the rod to cause a couple of welts. Then using his good camera he took the pictures.

Sarah swished the rod through the air a few times. "Bend over," she said sweetly yet wickedly. "Your marks are fading too."

He did, although he didn't like being punished nearly as much as she did. She birched him a little longer and harder than he had done to her, and finished it off with several harsh cuts. She picked up the camera and snapped several photos. Together they put the equipment away and went into the darkroom to develop the pictures.

When they were done they hung the new pictures up to dry and went to bed. They got out the album and reviewed the pictures of the night they first met and some of their other adventures. Then relaxed and mellow from the long night and the champagne, they made gentle tender love and fell asleep.

The next morning Sarah woke up feeling sensuous and aroused. It didn't take her long to figure out why. Mac was making love to her with his mouth. He was completely under the covers. She lifted the sheet and watched the top of his head as he worked his magic with teeth, tongue and lips. In a very short time she lost all conscious thought as sheer sensation took over. She came in a full crescendo, screaming loudly with the force of the orgasm. He came out from under the sheet and kissed her.

"Good morning," she said, kissing him passionately. "Thanks for the wake up."

"After last night it was the least I could do," he whispered against her mouth just before kissing her.

"So what's the most you could do?" She reached up and pulled him down to her.

"My dear, let me show you; actions speak louder than words."
And he did.

Chapter Twenty-two

You Bet Your Assets

The Paddle Club's First Annual *Casino Night* was promising to be a great success. Instead of going with the same old tired Las Vegas format, the club took advantage of the old-style decor in the clubhouse and chose to turn the rooms into an Old West Saloon and Dance hall. For the games, the members chose to concentrate on poker, blackjack and roulette.

Guest players bought their chips for money, and winnings were paid off in prizes. For members there were rewards and punishments, mostly consisting of various whippings and spankings. Because this event was open to the general public, only the actual prizes were handed out in public; any special awards, like spankings that members 'won' were saved for a private awards ceremony to be held after the general public went home.

The cash limit for buying chips was set at $100. There was a wide range of prizes donated by members and local businesses. They included everything from gag gifts and cheap knick-knacks for players who cashed in their chips with under $100, to much nicer gifts and prizes, such as gift certificates to local restaurants, cameras and stereos for the players who wound up with chips worth over $100.

Mixed in with some of the brightly wrapped gag gifts were also some pretty nice prizes; mainly free dinners for two at some of the better local restaurants. The guest who turned out to be the top winner of the night would get one of the nicer gifts, plus he or she would also get a new flat screen color television and a multi-disc DVD player.

The club member who wound up as the top winner had something special coming too. Nobody except Mac knew exactly what it was. In fact, some of the members weren't too sure if they really wanted to win it, and with good reason.

There was an old style ragtime piano, quite properly out of key, with Jerry at the keyboard. He wore a white shirt with a string tie and lacy garters on each arm. They also had dance hall girls with short, full skirts on their low cut, garish, satin dresses. They had long feather boas around their necks and bright lacy garters on their legs, holding up their fishnet stockings. The dance hall girls were Suzanne, Sherry and Toni.

Sarah was one of the dealers and she also circulated around the room carrying messages from one member to another. The other dealers included Mac and Clayton. Mario ran the roulette wheel. Edna and Annie were in a cash room acting as the cashiers. A smiling, cordial James helped Alan man the bar. They had several other members and a few off-duty police officers from the nearest town acting as security guards.

The *Casino Night* turned out to be a huge success, as expected. The large turnout was due partly to the fact that most of the non-member guests were curious about the club. They had all heard so many rumors and innuendoes for years that they were beside themselves with curiosity. Many of them had been in the building before; maybe when it was rented out for a private party such as a wedding reception or for another club's dance.

Some of the high schools in the area had even held their senior proms in the hall. If the clubhouse happened to be available when they needed it the school got it rent free, except for a fairly high, but fully refundable security deposit. This was different. This was the first real club function open to the general public, and the general public, which was dying of curiosity, came en masse.

Among the guests, much to Alan's delight was Sharon. She still hadn't decided to give the club a try but she felt comfortable enough with the club members that she had met at Alan's birthday party and the one party she had attended to give it a try. A special guest couple was also there, named Christie and Randy. They didn't know why they had been especially invited or even who had invited them, but they had accepted the invitation.

Suzanne and James studied them from across the room. Christie had the looks of a high school cheerleader; she had shoulder length blond hair, green eyes and she seemed to be bursting with energy. Watching her, Suzanne half expected her to do a back flip without warning. Her boyfriend Randy also had green eyes. The main thing that Suzanne noticed about Randy was the devilish mischief in his eyes. This one is a practical joker, Suzanne thought; he'd keep a girl on her toes.

Christie and Randy, Suzanne had learned, used a paddle to settle their baseball and football bets. She also knew that Christie had a deep, abiding hatred for baseball, while Randy was a baseball fanatic. James found an opportunity to speak to the couple quietly when they walked up to the bar for a drink.

"I heard you were especially invited to this event." He smiled warmly. "One of the members must have some reason to think you two might be interested in finding out more about joining the club. If you have any questions, feel free to ask."

"How would anyone know… ?" Christie's voice trailed off as she realized a friend of hers did know. The gossip.

"Hey! Don't be embarrassed, nobody's judging you." James winked. "You're among friends."

"Let me make something clear right now," Randy said. "I don't know what you've heard but we're not into real S & M, just friendly little spanking games."

"Also, we're not interested in having sex with other people," Christie added. "We're completely monogamous."

"You just described our club." Suzanne had walked over. "We're into spanking and sometimes we just skirt the edge of S & M. We have a dungeon in the basement but most of us never go down there. When we do, it's mostly for pretend, but sometimes a couple may really want to use the stuff down there. It may be less pretend for them. Also, sometimes pretend really does sting. We also don't exchange lovers. However we do exchange partners for spankings, if everyone involved agrees. And of course, no one is ever forced into anything."

"Have fun tonight and think about it. If you have any questions, feel free to ask anyone working here." James backed off, sensing that the couple wouldn't respond to pushing. "Except for the security officers, they're not club members, just off-duty city cops."

"And please," Suzanne told them, "don't discuss the club with other non-members."

Christie and Randy walked off to join the other guests. Although most of the guests at the casino were only interested in having fun, there were a few exceptions. The members were kept busy keeping the public from getting into arguments, drinking too much or damaging club property. The cashiers and barmaids had it fairly rough. Some of the men, fueled by the rumors, made crude passes at the three bar girls. The women handled these with gentle, good humor and a firm hand.

Only one man became so drunk that he was a real problem. An off-duty police officer, one of the men who had been hired for security, had to call for a squad car and have him arrested. That man was the only real problem of the night; there were no other arrests.

There was not much fooling around for the members while the guests were there. They didn't want to encourage any more rumors or even have anyone guess the truth. Still, many of the club members found moments to duck into one of the bedrooms off the kitchen for quick kisses and some hot and hasty foreplay. The distinctive sound of a hand smacking flesh was heard occasionally, sometimes followed by a gasp, but no one seemed to notice.

When the chips for the guests were cashed in, a sweet looking woman of about fifty was declared the big winner. She told James, who was acting as the master of ceremonies, that her name was Grace. She was small, fun and very feisty. She had salt and pepper hair and pale blue eyes.

"I'm really thrilled to win this television, mine is getting pretty old," she said, smiling broadly, then adding, "but I don't know anything about how to work a DVD."

Henry, a club member in his mid-fifties who owned a small appliance store had donated the prize. He volunteered to hook it up and show her how to use it. Their eyes met for a long moment. She looked at him with his soft brown eyes, slight paunch and gray hair, and softly thanked him for his helpful offer.

"But only on the condition that I can fix you and your wife dinner, to thank you for all your trouble," she added.

"It's no trouble, I'll enjoy doing it," he smiled, "and I'd love to come to dinner but I'm single."

"Not for long, Henry," Suzanne whispered in his ear as she passed him. "It looks to me like your single days are numbered."

She walked over to Sherry and Toni. "What do you want to bet that within six months we don't see Henry again?"

"Unless that sweet little lady is kinky." Sherry refused the bet. "But I agree, his goose is cooked."

"When their eyes met the air practically sizzled, it was so fantastic." Toni added, "Henry is a goner."

Clay and Mac came over. "What's going on?" Clay asked.

"Henry just fell in love with the lady who won the grand prize," Sherry told him, sliding her arms around his waist. "It was so romantic."

"If you want romance, just wait until I get you home," Clay murmured in her ear. Sherry smiled slyly in reply.

Christie and Randy were about to leave before another couple of club members went over to talk to them. It was Mac and Sarah. After a few minutes conversation, they explained that they were fairly new members of the club but that they enjoyed the friends they'd met so far.

Mac concluded the conversation by saying casually, "I have two extra tickets to the football game Sunday, would you two like to come with us?" He grinned guilelessly. "We could even have a friendly bet on the game."

"Not a bet involving…" Randy said.

"Oh no, we'll find something else for a wager," Mac said, "unless of course you'd like to bet…"

"No another bet will be just fine," Christie said, walking into Mac's trap.

Soon all the guests were leaving. The members and policemen directed traffic out of the parking lot. They made sure that any of the guests that had been drinking were not driving. The club had made arrangements for several of the local cab companies to send cabs to give free rides home to anyone who needed one.

When the crowd was cleared away for the most part, one off-duty policeman, a young and handsome officer named Robert Wilson took Suzanne aside.

"I know it's none of my business," he paused, clearing his throat, before he continued, "at least, I assume it's not any of my business, but I'm curious about the club. Can you tell me something about it?"

"Are you asking officially, as an officer of the law, or for yourself?" she asked, looking up at him.

"For myself. I mean, I'm not investigating you or anything like that," he answered honestly. "Of course, if you tell me you smuggle drugs, or guns, or hold human sacrifices or something ridiculous like that I would be forced to follow up on it."

"Fair enough, but if we're legal, don't tell anyone about us, deal?" She smiled and waited for his nod before continuing. "We are a club of people who enjoy playing spanking games that sometimes involve mild S & M. In our particular club we do not have orgies or even sex with anyone other than our own lovers or husbands, but we do play spanking games. All our games are voluntary, so there's no force or victimization involved. If you overheard us when we talk about our spankings to one another, you'd think we were heavily into real sadism and pain, but that's not so. We are into role playing and the suggestion of pain."

"How is that arousing?" he asked curiously. "I don't understand the appeal."

"Not everyone does, of course. Why should they?" she replied. "For me, it's a feeling of being out of control in someone else's hands, and just a little helpless. There's also a level of trust involved. I've also heard that getting a spanking brings all the blood to the genital area and makes the nerve endings more sensitive. It's also supposed to release pheromones. I don't know for sure and I don't care. I will tell you one thing though; you don't get domestic violence calls from our members. We don't let any abusive people or anyone who's really turned on by violence into the club."

"I've never had a call from anyone that I see here now," he admitted, smiling at her. "I don't know if I'd like it myself. But I'll give you a secret in return. Do you remember the city in Northern California that tried using spankings for traffic fines?" At her nod, he continued, "I was working as an officer in that town when that was going on. It's how I met my wife. I saw her at the station house when she was paddled for speeding. I went to her house and comforted her. Strictly against the rules, but I did. Then when I got a ticket myself, she returned the favor. I do remember one thing: in both cases we had exceptionally passionate sex that same night in spite of the pain, and my wife is not the kind of woman who would sleep with someone she just met, so maybe the paddle did stir something up. If you know what I mean."

"Maybe it had something to do with you too. The kind of man you are and, let's face it, your looks." Suzanne grinned at him. "Most women would want to get to know you better. I know I would if I didn't love James so much."

"Thanks." He grinned, a little sheepish.

"Back to the subject of spanking. Have you tried it since?" she asked. "For fun or teasing?"

"No, but we do both swat each other on the butt quite a bit," he replied thoughtfully.

"Then you're both probably kinky," she told him, smiling. "It might just be that the first time you were paddled it was much too frightening and severe for either of you to realize that a small part of you was turned on by it, even enjoyed it. You might want to try playing spanking games with your wife, but always quit if she tells you to."

"Maybe I will." He shook her hand.

"Are you flirting, wife?" James came up behind her and swatted her affectionately on her shapely butt. Suzanne and Mitch burst out laughing simultaneously.

"No," she managed between laughs. "I was just telling him that you were a wife beater. It sure was nice of you to give him that first-hand demonstration."

"And did you tell him that you return the favor? Hey Robert, I'm a battered husband," he said to the officer, who continued to laugh.

"I'd better go help with the cleaning. If you want to know more give me a call," Suzanne said as she took James by the arm. "Thanks for all your help tonight."

"I'll see you." He got into his car and left.

"I bet you all my chips that his wife has a nice pink butt tonight," she said.

"I'm not concerned with his wife's butt. I'm only interested in yours." He kissed her before they went inside. They had to help pay the members off by paddling their butts according to how many chips they wound up with. "And I know exactly what color your butt will be tonight."

"Pink?" she asked.

"More like flaming red." He swatted her right on the threatened butt as she went through the door.

"Who was the big winner among the members?" Suzanne asked.

"Well, we were discussing that before I came out to find you. There's a problem." James paused. "Since so many of the members were working and earned tips instead of gambling, we're debating if tips should count."

By the time they got inside, the issue had been decided. The rest of the members had voted and tips, indeed, would count! The tally was added up. For a while it seemed as if one of the three bargirls would "win" but as the last chips were counted, it turned out that James had won, edging out Suzanne by only $2.00 in chips.

"So strip down and lie on the floor, James," Mac said with a grin. "We have a little surprise for you."

James got into position good naturedly; after all he had been a member for several years, and he often enjoyed being on the receiving end of some of the punishments. However he knew this time the whipping would be worse, harder and longer than he was used to. He also knew that this time he would not be able to stop the proceedings by saying his code word or shouting "Stop!" That didn't bother him; after all, he trusted his friends. More or less.

James was surprised but not panicked when he felt straps being fastened around his ankles. In fact, he was enjoying the anticipation and the edge of apprehension he was feeling. The only moment of discomfort came when he realized he was being hoisted up until his hands were not even touching the ground. One of the male members caught his hands and tied them together. He was left hanging there as the rest of the members finished cleaning up the hall.

Just about the time he believed that every drop of blood in his body had finally drained into his head, the members came back. They had a wooden paddle, which was a mixed blessing to James. Paddles tended to cause less welting than a strap or lash, but because of that, punishments could go on longer without drawing blood or doing any real damage. He also knew from past experience that paddles with holes drilled into them hurt worse than paddles without holes. He looked. This one had several holes drilled into it. This would really sting.

Every club member took a turn giving James the dubious benefit of his or her years of practice and experience in wielding a paddle. He got anywhere from one to six blows from each of them. He swung back and forth with the force of the blows, yelling lustily at each one of them.

He had to yell for several reasons: First, it hurt! Second, he had learned long ago that with this bunch it wasn't smart to be too stoic. And besides, part of the fun for everyone was drawing a hearty reaction from the victim, and James was a very good victim.

When he was gently let down, he stood in the center of the group with one hand rubbing his glowing red ass.

"Gee, thanks guys. You shouldn't have gone to all that trouble for me. After all, since I only won by $2.00, it was practically a tie," James remarked slyly as he pulled his pants back on but leaving his fly unzipped because the punishment had caused him to get a painfully large erection.

Suzanne began to back quietly away from the group towards the door, sensing impending doom. All too soon she heard the words she knew were coming.

"Hey, that's right! Since Suzanne came so close to James' total, we ought to give Suzanne a little present too," someone suggested.

Although Suzanne knew she could take anything her friends could or would dish out, she was more than a little bit relieved to hear Mac say, "Yeah string her up, but she should only get about half as good a present as James. She was the runner-up so it would be sort of like a consolation prize."

Suzanne quietly removed all her clothes and lay down on the hardwood floor. She felt nervous as the straps were fastened around her slender ankles and she was pulled up into the air. She had never been hung upside down before. She felt weird hanging there, with her long, silky black hair brushing the ground. Her large breasts were stretched and hanging down. She wasn't left for a long time dangling like James had been; the club members started paddling her right away.

She felt herself swaying back and forth as the paddle landed on her rounded butt, but she soon learned a secret. The paddle hurt, but it didn't hurt too badly. Any blow hard enough to hurt very badly also caused her body to swing away from the force of it, thereby automatically defusing the full sting of the swing. She kept that secret very well because she yelled dramatically as each member gave her one swat, and then Mac and James both finished her off with five swats each.

"I'm going to get you when we get home!" she threatened James when she was finally lowered back to the floor. She retrieved her dress from the floor and started to put it on but James stopped her.

"You'd better believe it, dearie." James hugged her sliding his hands over her warm, tender ass and whispering into her ear, "You're going to get all of me." He took the dress from her hands and slid it very gently over her head. "Every single inch; every hot," he nipped her ear, "hard inch."

Chapter Twenty-three

A Real Entertaining Party

The *Casino Night* was still a hot topic of conversation at the next regular club party. Suzanne and James sat at a large table and were soon joined by Edna and Jerry, Clayton and Sherry, Toni and Mario, and Sarah and Mac. Jerry went to fetch drinks for everyone. They sat there talking and enjoying their drinks while they watched some of the activities going on round the room.

"Tonight should be fun," Suzanne told the new members. It was Toni and Mario's first regular party. "Mac and Sarah already know about this. They were there when Clay had the idea. We're having some skits tonight, along with whatever else happens. That's why the mike is on."

"What kind of skits?" Toni asked.

"You'll see," Clay said smiling, "one's starting right now."

There was a cocktail waitress at the bar; a petit brunette with a flirtatious manner. The only problem was — she was a lousy waitress. She spent far too long flirting with male customers, and not always single male customers. She ignored or was rude to female customers, forgot orders and also delivered the wrong drinks to several people. The topper was when she carelessly spilled drinks on two well dressed men, drenching their suits. The bartender called her over to the bar.

"Deliver these two martinis to table twelve for me." He turned away, busily mixing drinks. "Oh, and don't forget the olives."

"Where are they?" she asked.

"I'm stocking my supplies; you'll have to reach over the bar," he told her, not even turning back to look at her.

She stood on the bar rail and reached over the bar for the olives. Immediately the bartender grabbed her by both arms, pulling her high enough over the bar so that her feet no longer touched the ground. The two wet customers came over to stand on each side of her. Each man used one hand to raise her short frilly skirt.

"A dozen from each of us?" one man said to the other.

"I bet I can make my side a brighter red than yours," the other replied, "and the winner gets to give her an extra dozen."

The two men spanked her simultaneously, one on each side of her bottom. When they had each given her a dozen spanks, they pulled her panties down and argued over who had won the bet. Finally the winner gave her the final dozen swats and she was let up. Applause erupted around the room as the trio and the bartender took their bows.

James and Suzanne left the table to join in the fun.

"Are you enjoying yourselves so far tonight?" Clayton asked Toni. "This is your first regular party, isn't it?"

Toni smiled at him. "We are having fun."

"This should be a fun party tonight since everyone's here and," Clayton grinned, "we still have more entertainment planned."

Alan came over to join the table. "Hey Alan, where's Sharon? I thought she was going to give us a chance," Clay asked.

"She is," Alan replied, "but tonight she really did have to work."

"What about the Slave Auction?" Sarah asked. "Are Mac and I still going to buy her?"

"She agreed to it," Alan said, "but she's reluctant. I'm afraid…"

"Mac will take good care of her," Sarah interrupted him. "Don't worry."

"I will, you know," Mac added in. "Everything will be fine. Now which one of you needs a good, hard whipping?"

"I do, I do." Sherry stood up eagerly.

"Then get over to the bench bare-assed and in position, and wait for me," he ordered sternly.

Sherry moved quickly to comply. Mac turned to Sarah. "Lovey, go over and tie Sherry down for me, please. Blindfold her and lay out my assortment of toys next to her. I want to play *What's My Whipper*, with her. Then I want you to give yourself

169

over to Clay for a lesson in subservience."

"Yes, Mac." She moved off quickly.

Mac and Clay were the two most forceful tops in the club, followed closely by James. Jerry, while predominately a top, was so cheerful and friendly that the term just didn't seem to fit him.

"Jerry, why don't you try out my new flogger on Edna? It looks so severe but it really feels good," Mac suggested. "Ask Sarah which one I mean; she has it over there with the toys."

Jerry and Clay walked over to Sarah. She gave Jerry the flogger. It had a hundred very soft, thin lashes made of the finest suede. It looks horrific and made a satisfying smack when wielded on human flesh, but it stimulated and tingled instead of hurting. It took a real heavy hand to even begin to cause any real pain with the thing.

"Now Sherry," Mac said sternly, "I'm going to use several different toys on you. You have to describe what I'm using on you before I change to another, so wrong guesses will earn you extra smacks."

Upon hearing this, a small audience gathered. Mac picked up an oval paddle, leather on one side and mink on the other. Using the leather side he gave her two mighty smacks, one on each cheek. "What is it?"

"It's a paddle." Sherry got another pair of smacks.

"What is it made of?" Mac asked sternly.

"Leather?" Sherry guessed.

"Good girl." He got a brush and spanked her with it, without stopping. "Come on Sherry, what is this one?"

"A smaller paddle, aw, a hairbrush?"

Mac immediately switched to a cane. This time Sherry yelped out the answer almost immediately. Without hesitation, Mac reached for the birch.

After watching Sherry guessing what implement was being used on her backside for a while, Jerry tried the flogger out on his wife. She loved it. Mac was right. It made a real satisfying smack on her bottom but felt stimulating instead of painful.

Mac let Sherry up, hugged her and whispered to Clay. Clay

170

grinned and nodded. He turned to Sarah and wiggled one finger, gesturing her over. When Sarah was standing directly in front of him, Clay silently pointed to the floor. Instantly Sarah knelt at his feet, looking up at him with respect in her eyes.

Clay pointed at the implements, and Sarah stood up and walked over to them. She picked up a cane and looked over at Clay. He shook his head. She picked up another one, a little thicker and this time Clay nodded. He crooked his little finger again and she brought the cane to him. He gestured at her clothes and she stripped, folding each article of clothing as she removed it and carefully placing it on the nearest chair.

He pointed at the whipping bench and she got into position. Clay slashed the canes with cold efficiency, each stroke marking her with a long, red welt. She bore the cuts perfectly, without a sound and without any movement. When she had ten parallel welts, he snapped his fingers. She stood, walked over to Clay and knelt in front of him. He held out the cane and she kissed it. Then he gestured towards the corner and she stood there while various club members looked at the ten welts. Finally Clay snapped his fingers again and pointed at the pile of clothes and she dressed. He handed her the cane and she put it away. Then she came over to stand in front of him again.

Clay grinned and hugged her. "That was very good, my dear." Again the members applauded.

There were now two desks set up on the dais, with a thin partition between them. How long they had been there no one could say. Between Sarah and Sherry, they had all been too preoccupied.

Suzanne sat at one desk with cluttered piles of paper spread out in front of her. She was calmly talking on the phone, digging in her purse with one hand and gesturing with the other. Suzanne finally dug something out of her purse. It was a nail file. She began filing her nails. James walked over to the dais.

"Are you doing the filing?" he asked.

"Sure am, Boss man," she snapped her gum.

"I didn't mean your nails, Suzanne. Have you finished the

files?" James looked at her desk, noting the piles of papers. "I can see that you haven't. How about the letters I dictated? Are they ready for me to sign?"

"Not yet," Suzanne admitted. "Hey! You had a call."

"Who from? Where's the message slip?" James was losing his patience.

"I didn't write it down," Suzanne shrugged.

"You haven't typed my letters. You haven't done the filing. You didn't even take down my messages." James voice was low and ominous, "Is there anything you've done right today?"

"I remembered to make coffee," she said with indignation.

"Good," James said, "bring me some, at my desk."

"Can't," she said, grinning at him.

"Why not?" The question was cold.

"Drank it all." Suzanne went back to her nails.

"If you drank all that coffee," James asked exasperated, "how come you aren't wired from the caffeine? Like, for example, having enough energy to actually do some work?"

"Decaf." She looked away.

James walked over to his desk. He moved his chair away from the desk and into the center of the room. He turned on his intercom.

"Suzanne, in my office, now!" he ordered.

She came into his office and stood there. "Yeah?"

"I'm tired of your poor work habits and your attitude," James said sternly as he removed his suit jacket. He unbuttoned his cuffs and rolled up his sleeves. Then he sat in the chair. "Get over my knees. Now!"

"Hell, no!" She turned away.

In a flash, he jumped up and grabbed her. He dragged her over to his chair, sat down and pulled her over his knees. Ignoring her wiggling and struggling, he worked her skirt up over her behind and pulled down her panties. Then he began to spank her with loud walloping smacks, right in the area framed by her garter belt and straps. She squirmed and cursed him out, causing him to hit her even harder.

Eventually her bottom really began to sting and she reached back with both hands to cover her bottom. Turning her head to face the audience, she winked and stuck out her tongue. James grabbed both hands with his and began to spank her much harder. It was one helluva spanking and when he stopped, the members applauded again.

The group of friends sat down for another round of drinks. Soon the soft rock music stopped. Someone had interrupted the usual soft rock music and put on opera. There was a slightly paunchy man of about thirty-five on the dais. With his back to the crowd he dropped his pants and underwear and bent over the back of a chair, bare bottom. A young woman picked up a birch rod just as a song began. Soon, the man was being birched while singing along with the tape. He had a beautifully trained voice and perfect pitch. He also never missed a note of *The Toreador Song* from the opera *Carmen* during the entire birching.

When the song was finished the birching stopped. The man stood up and pulled up his pants. As the members applauded he took a bow.

Seeing this, even Sarah and Mac were stunned. "Does this happen often?" Sarah's voice came out as a whisper.

"Not really." James winked. "It's only the second time I've heard him sing because he's usually on tour."

The group relaxed and enjoyed their drinks before anyone realized that Clay and Sherry were gone. Even as they looked around Clay walked up to the mike, in costume.

"I met Sherry when we were in a play together. So tonight we're going to reprise a scene from the roles that brought us together."

Much to the surprise and delight of everyone, they performed the spanking scene from *Kiss Me Kate*.

Chapter Twenty-four

Training For A New Little Slave

How Sharon's lover talked her into it, she never really knew. Maybe it was because Alan was such a kind, gentle man while still a very exciting lover. Maybe it was because the idea was so wild and outlandish it couldn't fail to seem unreal, and to be intriguing. Maybe it was because it was for charity.

For a long time Alan had been trying to talk her into joining the Paddle Club. He had introduced her to some of the members, and he had taken her to a regular party and the club's *Casino Night*. He claimed the club was all fairly innocent, more fun and titillation than pain. It was also, he had explained, not a sex club for swingers. For the most part club members were monogamous and romantically involved with their own spouses or lovers. Spankings however, were more open. Members frequently exchanged partners for spanking, paddlings and whippings. From what Sharon had seen most of the members were very nice people.

So far Sharon and Alan had not played any spanking games, not even in private. Sharon was what Alan called a "spanking virgin" because no one, not even her parents, had ever hit or spanked her. The fact that a gentle, quiet man like her lover thought it would be really fun to spank her totally shocked and mystified her.

The fact that he wanted to put her up as a slave at a Paddle Club *Slave Auction* caused her to feel shivers up her spine but the thought of it also secretly intrigued her, inwardly arousing her curiosity. She trusted Alan so how bad could it be? Oh well, she thought as she agreed, curiosity killed the cat; in fact it had killed several cats.

The way Alan explained it to her she would be put entirely at the mercy of a total stranger, except for one thing: Each 'slave' made up a list of things they would not submit to. The masters would know in advance what boundaries they could take a slave to. It was agreed that no one was going to cross those boundaries.

There were three basic levels of slaves listed in the catalog: BRONZE SLAVES, which he wanted Sharon to be, were the lowest level of slaves. They were to be lightly punished only with hands or paddles, no whips, and there would be no bruises, blood or any other injuries. No tight or extended bondage, and no excessive humiliation.

SILVER SLAVES were punished more and the paddles would be harsher, drilled with holes to sting more and sometimes even whips could be used. They were also tied up more often, tighter and left that way longer.

GOLD SLAVES were open to all physical punishments and bondage in any way, limited only by the rule that no real injuries could be inflicted.

The auction was to take place on Thursday evening at the beginning of a three-day weekend. Her enslavement would begin immediately after the auction and end Sunday at midnight.

Sharon stood on the pedestal, shivering slightly, naked except for a g-string, a tiny matching bra, a blindfold and a flowing cape. Her long blond hair was gathered roughly on top of her head. She had bronze slave bracelets on both wrists and her hands were tied behind her back.

She was so scared she was almost numb when she felt the attendants removing her cape. Soon their hands were on her body while the auctioneer was extolling her virtues. She was turned around and felt her buttocks being stroked and handled. Although they left her tiny bra on, she felt almost as if she were just an object as her breasts were very impersonally lifted, pushed together and lightly stroked.

She felt her hair being unpinned, felt it falling to flow around her white shoulders. Her chin was lifted and the blindfold was removed. She was told to look at the crowd so that they could see her face and eyes. Then the bidding began and she was blindfolded again. Behind the blindfold she felt scared, humiliated, objectified and very defiant. She shuttered as she heard the gavel slam down.

A collar was fastened around her neck and the cape was put back on. She was told briefly by Alan to be silent and obey. She was led, still blindfolded, to a car and helped into it. After a short drive, she was helped out of the car and into a building. Her unseen Master led her down some stairs into a slightly cool room. He removed her cape and bra but he left her g-string in place.

"I am your new Master; you will serve me and my wife, your mistress, until Sunday at midnight. Here are the rules: You will not speak to me unless I tell you to. In fact, you will not speak at any time at all unless I tell you to." He paused, then continued with just a trace of kindness in his voice. "You will be treated according to the rules you agreed to. I know that this is your first time as a slave so I will be very gentle, patient and careful of you, but nevertheless you will be punished twice a day beginning tonight, whether you misbehave or not. You will wait in position for me to give you a morning spanking at 8:00 AM. You will also wait in position for your evening punishment at midnight. If I do not feel like punishing you myself, my wife, my butler or my cook will perform the task. It does not matter who does it; to them, it's just another chore. You will obey every order I give you instantly and without comment. Any order from my lady, my butler or my cook is the same as if it came from me. You will also be punished during the day if you misbehave, and even sometimes if I just feel like punishing you for nothing other than my own amusement. If you are being punished for misbehaving, I will tell you that you are a bad slave and you will ask me, with downcast eyes and great humility in your own words, to beat you into submission. When I finish beating you, you will thank me for taking the time to give you the beating and ask me, no, *beg* me, to beat you again. During these beatings and your morning and evening punishments you will say 'Thank you very much, Master' after every slap of my hand or stroke of the paddle. If I'm beating you just for my amusement however, you will not speak at all, but you will squirm and moan and give me a real show of how much you, um, enjoy the punishment."

The Master paused briefly before saying, "Now you will receive your first punishment. For this punishment you will act as though it's a punishment for misbehavior by asking for it and by thanking me for each and every blow." His voice grew colder and more commanding. "Take one step forward and bend over."

She hesitated; her fear seemed to paralyze her.

Her Master barked, "Now!"

She felt terrified at hearing the request and being blindfolded only added to her fear, but with trembling legs she stepped reluctantly forward and bent at the waist. She wound up lying from the waist up on a soft, padded table. Her Master told her to ask for her punishment.

In a trembling voice she said, "Please punish me, Master."

He directed her hands to a soft rope and told her to hold onto it tightly or she would be tied down. She felt bizarre lying there, scared and helpless. The g-string was no protection for her bottom and she was very conscious of the cool air blowing on her naked buttocks, waiting for the beating to begin.

It started; a light teasing flicker of a soft string whip that didn't hurt at all. As the soft strings descended over and over, she began to relax. She thought that teasing flicker was the full punishment. Alan had been right when he told her it was all a game.

Soon her Master began to use his hands gently, lightly, all over her body except on her buttocks. Finally he spanked her buttocks gently, building very slowly to a slight tingling. Her butt turned a slight pink. A faint stirring of shock ran through her as she realized that she was really enjoying this.

"Now we begin. Remember to thank me after every stroke," her Master told her, his uncanny sense of timing telling him that she was ready.

Suddenly she was being spanked, really spanked, hard and fast with her Master's hand. She barely managed to get the phrase out after every spank. It went on for a long time. It stung and the slaps landed with a loud clap but it was not really painful at all. Finally he stopped.

She lay there breathing heavily and feeling very relieved when suddenly, for the first time in her life, she felt a paddle descend on her tight little ass. It was hard and fast, and a lot more painful. She tried to repeat the phrase after each blow but sometimes she fell behind.

"You failed to thank me for every blow and it took too long for you to get into position in the first place. However other than that, for the first punishment you did alright so I will be merciful and not punish you for your obvious imperfections. Now thank me for taking the time and energy to give you such a good beating. Remember, you are always supposed to beg me to beat you again."

"Thank you for giving of your time and energy by beating me. I'm sorry for my imperfections," she managed, breathing heavily. "Please Master, beat me again."

"Alright, little slave, since you ask so prettily, I will." He always knew when to keep going.

The paddle descended again and again as he beat her a dozen more harsh stinging blows. This time she forgot to say, "Thank you Master" for the first blow but he gently reminded her.

When he stopped paddling her she said without any prompting, "Thank you for giving me such a good beating. Please beat me again."

"I will, my greedy little slave, but not now," her Master told her quietly. She felt him kiss her on top of her head. "You may stand up."

He gently removed her blindfold for the first time. She gasped as she looked around the room. It was obviously a dungeon; there was no other word for it. It was set up in a basement. Her new Master stood in front of her; he was tall and well built, dressed in black leather. His face was covered by a mask but she could tell he was muscular and had blue eyes. She had the impression that he was very handsome. Next to him, dressed in black silk and wearing a black mask was a woman. She was short and had red hair and bright green eyes.

The Master spoke into the air, "How did you like that?"

The question seemed directed behind her.

She was shocked to hear his mistress' voice reply, "I thought it was great. Did the slave enjoy it?"

Her Master said, "You may reply."

"I'm not too sure, it was too strange and I was so scared. It really hurt too, but at least it wasn't as bad as I feared," she replied softly.

"You may lie on the bed; you have no duties until dinner. I will ring for you to come serve me and then you will be fed. I will require your assistance to bathe, then that will be all until bedtime. You do remember what I said to do at bedtime?"

"Yes, Master." She lay down on the bed.

"Now it's time for my second slave to come forward." The Master's voice was harsh and commanding.

Sharon was surprised to see her lover, Alan, step into the room. He was nude except for a g-string. He did not have on a blindfold. Without hesitation he placed himself in position for a beating. This time the Master did not start easily. He used a larger, heavier paddle which he swung hard and fast, so fast that her lover had a hard time thanking the Master for each blow.

When he finished the paddling and her lover requested more, the Master refused, saying that he would ring for both of them at dinner time. He left her lover tied to a ring set high into the concrete wall, his feet barely touching the hard concrete floor.

She lay on the bed, gently rubbing her tender bottom and looking at her lover. She saw his bright red buttocks and realized that she was enjoying the feeling of having a shared experience; she had even enjoyed watching him being paddled.

"Did you really enjoy watching me get paddled?" she asked out loud, forgetting that she was forbidden to speak.

Immediately a door opened and the Master strode in. "You spoke; you are a bad slave!"

She was shocked. "Please punish me, Master."

"I will, but I will not beat you this time." He tied her to the wall with her hands stretched above her head. "You may thank me for my mercy."

"You are truly merciful, Master. I thank you," she whispered.

Just about the time her arms started to ache, a man dressed in a tuxedo came in and untied her lover and then let her down. He instructed them to follow him, explaining that he was the Master's butler for the weekend.

"My name is Randy. My duties for this weekend are to direct you in how to serve the Master and occasionally to give you the morning or evening spanking if the Master directs me to do so." Seeing the surprise on her face, the butler said, "You have my permission to ask me a question."

"Did he buy your services at the auction too?" she asked.

"No, little slave." The butler smiled ruefully. "I lost a football bet."

The butler introduced them to the cook, a lovely blond named Christie who gave them their serving costumes. Sharon was given a lacy white apron with a see-thru bib to wear over her g-string, and a lacy cap. She was instructed to put her hair up, then put on the tiny cap. Alan was given a tuxedo jacket and a black bow tie to wear with his g-string. The butler directed them on their duties in serving meals to the Master, his lady and his guests.

It was strange serving dinner to four people who were all wearing masks, but Sharon tried to do a good job.

As she served the hot soup the female guest remarked, "Your new slave is beautiful. She has a lovely behind. May I spank her?"

"Of course, my slave is yours to torment." He smiled before he instructed the slave, "Do not put the soup down, just walk over to the right side of the lady's chair and ask her to spank you very hard, then turn your back to her and lean slightly forward, sticking your butt out. You will be spanked by the lady. If you spill as much as one drop of soup you will also be severely beaten by the butler after dinner. When she is done spanking you, you will thank her for her time and effort and continue serving the soup without any further comment."

She followed her Master's instructions, walking over to the lady and saying, "Please madam, would you give me a very hard spanking?"

The little slave was surprised that the lady did not answer immediately. Instead the guest reached out and stroked her cheek then trailed her hand gently down the slave's body. The lady then slid her hand around the slave to glide gently over the slave's buttocks. All this was shocking to the slave, who had never been touched by a woman.

"Yes, indeed I will," the lady finally replied. "I will give you the spanking you deserve."

Awkwardly the little slave turned around and leaned slightly forward, timidly sticking her behind out.

"It's a great honor that the lady wants to punish you, little slave. Please give her a good target," her Master said. "Stick your behind well out, and be proud of it."

The little slave complied as best she could. Immediately the woman began spanking her with quick, loud slaps. The spanking was fairly hard but it was fast, and all the spanks landed on one cheek. Soon she paused and looked at the male guest; he shook his head smiling, and she continued onto the other cheek. The little slave fought hard not to spill any soup, and to her relief she succeeded.

"Thank you for doing me the honor of giving me a good, hard spanking," she murmured, her eyes downcast.

She continued around the table to the male guest.

He sampled his soup and complained, "The soup is cold!"

Her Master spoke instantly, his words sending a chill down the little slave's spine. "I'm awfully sorry. Would you like to punish my lowly slave for her laxness in failing to serve you hot soup?"

The male guest gently rubbed the slave's still warm buttocks. "No, she's not worth the effort."

The little slave was surprised to realize that she was insulted, and something else. Was she disappointed? She was relieved, of course, as the male guest looked extremely stern. She had a feeling that a spanking from him would be very painful indeed, by far the harshest she would have ever received. Still she was insulted and more than a little let down. She was almost pouting as she served the soup to the Master's lady. Catching her expression the group grinned to themselves; truly there was more than one way to punish a slave.

"Very well, I'll add her punishment for the poor service to her nightly dose, if you wish," the Master offered.

"No need," the guest replied. "Now that I think of it, I realize that my wife was at fault for delaying the slave in performance of her duties. I think I'll punish my wife instead."

The rest of the meal passed without incident.

Chapter Twenty-five

The Slave's Training Continues

After dinner the Master and his lady led the group down to the basement and chained both of his slaves to the walls, but this time, not with their arms raised painfully high above their heads.

Before long, the butler brought them both bowls of stew and fresh bread. He unchained them and let them eat. He also showed them where there was a button they would be able to reach if they wanted to signal him that they needed to relieve themselves during the night. He also warned them that there would be severe consequences if they ever used that button.

He also reassured them that all the manacles were rigged to the building's alarm system so that they would be automatically released if there was a fire or an emergency. After they ate he chained them back up and the slaves rested; as well as they could in their chains until the butler came to get them to help the Master and his lady with their nightly baths. The male slave was assigned to draw the baths and lay out the couple's bedclothes and robes, and wait with the towels to dry them after their baths.

The Master and his mistress were both still wearing masks. The little slave was assigned to wash the Master. She lathered her Master timidly working her way over his solid body and only hesitating when she came to his genitals. At the Master's soft order, she washed him there too. In fact, at his order she spent quite a long time washing him there.

After his bath, she dried him and helped him put on his bedclothes while Alan bathed the mistress. The butler then led the two slaves downstairs.

It was already midnight, so at the butler's whispered reminder, the little slave put herself into position for her nightly punishment while her lover watched. Then he placed himself into position. She shivered nervously. Soon the Master and mistress came down.

He said, "I'm extremely pleased with both of you but especially you, my little slave. You have made great progress for someone who has never been under anyone's discipline or domination. You are very trainable. Tonight, as a reward, I will give you your harshest taste of punishment yet."

Without saying anything to the Master, the little slave questioned herself about how getting her harshest punishment yet could possibly be considered a reward.

Immediately he fulfilled his promise. He did give her a long warm up. The little slave was so new to this game that she barely appreciated how patient he was with her. Then he paddled her hard and long. She barely made it through the first dozen before she started to have trouble saying the required sentence after each blow. After two dozen, she was stripped of her g-string, blindfolded and chained hand and foot to the bed, with her red, hot bottom facing up.

She heard her lover getting his nightly beating, and then he was beside her, chained, and just out of her reach.

"You two may talk for fifteen minutes without penalty," her Master said as he left the room. "After that, any talking will be punished."

"Are you all right?" Alan asked. "I really didn't realize he would take it to this extreme."

"He's paddled me hard enough to really smart and sting but he hasn't really hurt me, and his rules are clear. It seems fairly easy to follow them, but it's so strange," Sharon whispered, "I feel so helpless. I also feel so insignificant, like an object."

"Remember, you are also being cared for, like a very valuable object," her lover reminded her, "and remember that ultimately, you are in control. You have already set your terms. You are also safe; you may be hurt but you will not be injured, either physically or sexually. Of course, the money the slave auction raised is going to AIDS research."

"I also feel a strange kinship to you, closer than making love somehow, by hearing and watching you getting beaten and knowing exactly what you are feeling. It's sort of like the bonds people must form when they survive a terrible experience together," she confessed to him.

"But is it a terrible experience?" he asked gently. "Are you sorry I talked you into this?"

"Yes. No. I'm not sure. I don't know," she stuttered her reply. "All I can say for sure is that I'm certainly not bored."

"You may not know for sure how you feel until months after this weekend is over," her lover said softly. "But I'll tell you one thing: you were disappointed when the male guest refused to spank you, and it showed."

"Did it?" she said quietly. "I was disappointed and I felt insulted. It was the strangest feeling. Very odd."

They fell silent as they heard a voice say, "Stop talking now."

They were both stiff when the butler, now in slacks and a polo shirt came to unlock their chains at six o'clock on Friday morning. He helped them up, and waited while they stretched and used the bathroom. Then he directed the male slave into the shower and ordered him to raise his hands up so he could be handcuffed to the wall.

The female slave was ordered to use the hand held shower, harsh soap and a stiff scrub brush to wash him, including his hair. She was also instructed to be careful to try not to arouse him, but that proved impossible. She dried her lover off, using a blow dryer to dry his hair.

Next she was chained to the wall with her arms stretched high above her head and harshly scrubbed. Her lover washed her hair. He dried her off and brushed and blow-dried her long hair. They were both given clean g-stings to wear.

The butler took them to the kitchen where mouthwatering smells of bacon and coffee filled the air. The slaves were not given coffee or bacon and eggs; they were given bowls of oatmeal and glasses of milk.

After breakfast, the two slaves were instructed to clean up the kitchen and then taken back downstairs to wait for their morning punishments.

This morning the mistress used her hands to give the slaves a brisk, but not overly harsh spanking. When it was over, both of them had warm, rosy bottoms.

The mistress had them dress in silky underwear that they pulled right over their g-strings. She also had pants for the male slave and a black dress for the female. She ordered the slave to put the starched maid's apron over the dress. She assigned them both light housekeeping chores, mainly dusting and arranging flowers.

Around midmorning, the Master found fault with the female slave. He claimed she wasn't getting all the dust and that she was being lazy.

He told her, "You're a bad slave."

She quickly remembered the required lines. "Please beat me Master, and make me into a good slave."

"I will. Bend over the sofa," he pointed and instructed.

He stood behind her and raised her skirt up. Then he gently, very, very slowly lowered her silky underwear. He instructed the male slave to bring the small paddle from the basement.

It seemed like it took him forever as she waited in suspense for the punishment to begin. Finally her lover returned with the paddle. The Master used it with cold efficiency on her; not especially severely but without comment or buildup.

When he stopped, she followed the protocol he had established and said, "Thank you for the beating you have given me, please beat me again."

Immediately, without hesitation or comment, he began again, this time just a little harder, just a little faster. This time when he was finished and she made the required request, he refused.

The rest of the morning passed without incident. After serving lunch and then being fed bread and stew, they were put to work cleaning the kitchen and starting to get everything ready for dinner.

Early in the afternoon while they were polishing silver, the Master called the male slave into the living room. He was ordered to lower his pants and kneel on the floor while the

Master straddled him facing his butt and beat him with a long leather strap, the hard blows coming almost straight down on his backside. It was a long and severe beating, and the slave squirmed and moaned, showing just how much he appreciated and enjoyed the degrading punishment.

Later the female slave was ordered to kneel on the sofa and stick her butt up, in position for a beating. The Master's lady paddled her over her clothes, and kept telling her to move and moan more.

"Really stick out that butt, and work it!" she said. "I'm putting a lot of effort into this. Show me you appreciate my effort."

The slaves were given a break and tied to their bed, before they dressed in their serving costumes and went upstairs to serve dinner.

That night they were given their evening spanking by the butler; it was stinging but not overly harsh. Saturday morning they were again awakened and fed by the butler. He watched again as they washed each other. At the appointed time he gave them the morning spankings, this time with a paddle. The paddling was a little harder but still not very harsh. The male slave was given a clean g-string. The female was given a g-string, a corset and nylons. The corset left her nipples and buttocks bare.

They were taken to the Master.

He said, "I have something for you to wear." He put a pair of nipple clamps on her; they were not very tight put they felt very strange. "If you take these off or even touch them, I will punish you very severely."

The sensation of the clamps on her tender nipples was incredible, almost but not quite painful. Being forced to wear them was strange. Being forbidden to touch them was an exquisite torment. It brought home to her more than anything else did so far that she was under this man's control.

The Master spoke. "Let's go outside. You both need some exercise and... stimulation." He handed both of them coats.

They were taken out to the Master's stables and ordered to clean the stalls. At one point both of them were bent over the hay and soundly spanked just for fun. The Master used his hand on the little slave and a leather riding crop on her lover.

Then the Master took them both into his small circular arena with a thirty-foot diameter. It was completely enclosed since working horses could be distracted during early stages of their training.

The female slave went first, running around the circle beside her Master, while her lover knelt in the center. Her Master paddled her butt as she ran, with her hands locked behind her neck. Next it was her lover's turn to run. The Master used a long whip to drive him on, leaving his butt and flanks covered with long thin welts.

Back inside the house, they were both chained to the bed for a rest before lunch, with the nipple clamps still on. A pair of clamps was also placed on her lover, and the Master told her that his were tighter and more severe. She ached to touch her breasts; the clamps made her very sensitive, but she was chained so that she had no use of her hands.

She had to keep the clamps on until they were unchained to serve lunch and clean the kitchen. Then the Master gave them each a sound spanking across his knee just for the fun of it. They spent the remainder of the afternoon serving the mistress. First the female slave served as her footstool while her lover acted as a snack tray, on his hands and knees holding the mistress' food and drinks on his back. Unfortunately for him, he spilled a drink. He was punished severely with the heavy paddle.

That night it was the cook who gave them the evening spanking, quickly, impersonally and only moderately painful.

Sunday morning, the last morning, after the butler fed and watched them bathe, the Master gave them the morning punishment himself. He used his hands. There was once again a warm up but it built quickly. He spanked her harshly. Very harshly. He left no doubt that someone could be punished severely without the use of a paddle or a whip of any kind. The spankings both lasted a long, long time and left both slaves with bottoms that were very red, very hot and very stinging.

They were put to work cleaning the house from top to bottom, and before noon each of them had been paddled smartly for some small misbehavior. Each time when the slave made the required request for a second beating it was granted with a vengeance.

They were once more exercised in the small pen, then allowed to rest until it was time to serve their Master's dinner. This time they were not fed. They were groomed again, and again they both had the nipple clamps on. They were tied with their hands over their heads. They waited like that, stiff and hungry, in a house filled with the aroma of good food. They had been fed plenty, but they had not been given anything to eat but bread, stew, oatmeal and milk since Thursday at noon.

At seven o'clock the mistress came and got them and to their surprise, gave them a special meal: succulent steaks, salads, cheesy garlic bread, baked potatoes and fine wine. She told them their final punishment would be at eleven, so that they would be free by midnight. This would be the harshest punishment yet, she warned. They savored the fine meal. Later they assisted the Master and mistress with their baths and then went down to the basement to get ready for the final beating.

The butler came down and gave them both a fairly hard spanking, then the cook used the paddle with moderate severity on the slaves. Finally, the Master and mistress came down.

"Before the Master and I give you your final punishments, we have decided that you should each take a turn punishing each other," the mistress said. "Alan, you will punish Sharon first. You may place her in any position you wish and use your hand or a paddle; it's up to you."

Alan moved to sit on the wooden chair. He directed Sharon to face him and straddle his legs, resting her thighs on his, and laying her head on his shoulder next to his neck. He held her gently and lovingly with one arm around her waist, while his free hand stroked her soft butt. Then the spanking began. It was long and loud; every so often he changed hands and spanked the other side of her ass. Finally, he put her into the traditional position and with a series of hard blows, he was finished. Now it was her turn.

Sharon was a novice at the spanking game. She had never given anyone any kind of spanking. However she certainly rose to the occasion. Looking around the room at the various implements of torment, she chose a heavy leather paddle. She positioned Alan on his hands and knees on the floor and sat on him, straddling him and facing his white ass. Without fanfare, she paddled him slowly and thoroughly, covering his entire buttocks and working on his flanks and thighs. She knew that when she finished it was time for her to face her final punishment from the Master and mistress. It took her a long time to finish.

The mistress commenced. First, she started by dealing with the female slave, spanking her very severely with a wooden paddle, and for a very long time. Then she turned her attention to the male slave, spanking him with the same paddle as hard as she could.

Next, while the female slave watched, the Master paddled the male slave very hard and for a very long time, finishing with about a dozen slashing cuts with a heavy leather strap.

The female slave knew the Master was saving her punishment for last for a reason – it would be monumental! She was stripped completely naked except for the nipple clamps. She was tied tightly and blindfolded. The Master used the wooden paddle as he paddled her harder than anything she had ever felt before, starting slowly and building up speed. Harder and faster still.

Finally he stopped and said two words. "Leather strap?" It was a question.

To her own shock, she nodded. Her Master whipped her severely with the leather strap. He gave her about a dozen slashing cracks of the leather. For the first time, she had a few welts and bruises. It was over. Her blindfold was removed. The Master, mistress, the cook and the butler went upstairs.

At the landing the Master turned and said, "I hope you both enjoyed your weekend. We all worked very hard to make it eventful and exciting for you. You may leave whenever you wish, or you may both stay here for a while and use the bed. Whatever. Your street clothes are in the closet there, and your car is in the driveway. Good-bye."

Sharon was shocked to realize that she had still not seen their faces.

Chapter Twenty-six

Spanked On The High Seas

Since the club was so couples oriented it was extremely rare for an odd number of people to be initiated to the club, but shortly after the *Slave Auction* that's exactly what happened. There were three prospective new members. Sharon was still hesitant but she decided to join, at least to give the club a try for Alan's sake. After all, she'd survived the slave weekend, hadn't she? Although she wasn't ready to say if she really liked it or not, she had daydreamed about it several times. The other new couple was Christie and Randy, the cook and butler from Sharon's weekend as a slave. Unbeknownst to Sharon, it would be her former Master, Mac, serving as the evening's host.

Sharon was really surprised to see Randy and Christie again, and more than a little embarrassed. She saw them from across the room and waited for them to come towards her.

"Hi." She blushed. "It's ah, nice to see you again."

"Hey!" Randy teased. "You don't seem all that happy to see us. You should at least try to sound like you mean it. Weren't we good to you?"

"Don't let him bother you, Sharon," Christie added, gently taking her arm. "After all, we're all in the same boat tonight and I, for one, am glad to see a familiar face."

"Besides, I think I owe you two a little payback." Sharon regained her spirits as Alan walked over to join her. "And you two aren't the only ones. I just wish I knew who my former Master and mistress were."

"You'll figure it out soon enough," Christie assured her. "They're both pretty hard to miss."

Sharon did indeed figure it out as soon as she saw Mac and Sarah. Everything about them was so obvious; she felt foolish that she hadn't recognized them from the *Casino Night*. In fact, it was a wonder they had bothered with wearing the masks at all that weekend. His superb build and blazing blue eyes, and her bright red hair and sparkling green eyes gave them away instantly.

Her Master's identity was confirmed when she heard his soft whisper in her ear, "Hello, my little slave. Long time no spank. Miss me?"

She turned around, surprised to see Mac standing so close beside her. He smiled warmly at her and handed her a glass of champagne before slapping her sharply on the ass.

"Hi Alan." He turned to Alan. "I see Sarah and I didn't manage to scare her off after all."

"Hi Alan, Sharon," Sarah greeted the pair. "I'm glad to see you two again. Welcome to the club, Sharon."

They followed the tradition of having the new members whip the club members first. To Sharon's surprise, she liked it. She realized quickly that she liked giving whippings a lot more than being on the receiving end. Randy and Christie both did okay at giving whippings too. The old members had a real hot time of it. Almost all of them, no matter how experienced, were sitting gingerly after that part of the initiation

After another glass of champagne for everyone, it was time for Sharon to undergo her initiation. All through her whipping Sharon struggled. She flinched and squirmed, her blue eyes as big as an owl's, but she didn't scream or make any outcry.

"That cane sure hurts more than a paddle!" she exclaimed, gently rubbing her butt. She laid face down on the padded chaise.

After a break for refreshments, Christie was next. She bore her initiation well, yelling only a little. Once she had moved away from the whipping bench, there was another short break for refreshments and Randy was next. His mischievous smile faded as soon as the birching began. He yelled much louder than Christie had, and tears formed in his eyes. He apparently was luckier at betting on football than Christie was, and because of that he'd had less practice at being the person on the receiving end of the whip.

Alan rode home with Sharon in the limousine. He carried her gently into the house and up to the bed.

"Thank you for joining the club." He kissed her. "I know you're still not too sure about it."

"I think it's going to be okay." She grinned up at him. "But I realized something tonight."

"What's that?" He looked innocent.

"I like doing the spanking and whipping a lot better than being on the receiving end," she said firmly.

"Somehow I already knew that," he grinned, "when you paddled me on our last night as slaves."

"Did I hurt you?" She was wide-eyed and concerned.

"Not enough for me to ask you to stop," he told her. "But don't think you're going to get away with that all the time."

"I just wish I'd gotten my hands on that former Master of mine." She dreamed of getting a bit of revenge. "I'd love to have him under my whip."

"Be glad you got to whip Sarah," he warned her. "Mac is seldom on the receiving end. He's a complete Dom. Did he ever really hurt you?"

"No. It was weird now that I look back on it. He always seemed to know just how far to take things, both the slavery and the punishments. I felt like I was taken to the edge of my limits and yet there were no bruises, no real pain and no real humiliation."

"That's why I asked Mac to make sure he bought you," Alan confessed. "He's got a real knack for reading people. It's almost uncanny. He always knows how far to go."

"I've been wondering why you wanted someone else to give me my first spanking. It was almost as weird as if you had wanted someone else to take my virginity," Sharon said. "Tell me, why?"

"I knew that Mac would know if you were interested, and he would know how to read your feelings, to make everything right for you," Alan explained. "Besides, I'm really a sub. I'm a better victim than a Master. I don't know if you realized it, but being a

Master was a lot of work. He had to find things to keep you occupied all weekend, both work for you to do and ways to make sure that you got into trouble often enough to deserve punishment."

"I never thought about it like that. Well, at least we make a good pair." She reached up to him, a wicked gleam in her eyes, "I'm a Dom and you are a sub, my sub. Now make love to me and make it good or I'm going to have to make things very painful for you."

"Yes my love, my mistress." He lowered his mouth, hovering just slightly over her. He slid his arms under her legs and lowered his mouth to the moist junction of her silky thighs. "I'll do my best."

The next day they went sailing. Sharon packed a picnic basket with lunch and a few surprises, plus she stocked the boat's galley and they set off to find a little privacy on the high seas. They found a quiet cove off one of the islands near Santa Barbara and dropped anchor.

Sharon luxuriated in the feel of the warm sun on her bare back as she lay on the deck. "Hey Alan!" she called.

"What?" his voice drifted up from the cabin.

"Get your worthless behind out here and rub some sun block on me," she ordered. "You'd better not let me burn."

Alan was shocked at the tone she was using; it was so different from her usual loving voice. He hurried up on deck and began to rub lotion on her. He worked his way gently down from the nape of her neck to the base of her spine before she stopped him.

"Do my legs next, and do a good job of it," she ordered sternly, rolling over.

He moved down to her toes, rubbing the lotion with painstaking care and gentleness over her feet, ankles and calves.

"Now do my thighs," she moaned. "Be sure to get the inside of my thighs."

He smoothed the sunscreen on her thighs very slowly. The front of her thighs, the outside, even lifting her legs at the knee and smoothing lotion on the backs of her thighs. Finally he moved to the inside of her thighs and spent a delicious eternity moving ever so slowly up from her knees towards the moist center of her femininity, his fingertips lightly teasing the crotch of her swimsuit. She shivered.

Abruptly he stopped and asked her to roll over. He began at the small of her back rubbing lotion in tiny, gentle circles. She lifted herself up and he slid the bottom of her swimsuit off, and unfastened the top half.

Finally, he moved to her buttocks. He rubbed the lotion gently over her with devastating thoroughness, even working his way into the crack between her nether cheeks. His fingers brushed her anus and found her vagina. Then he poured a large glob of lotion on the crest of each check of her buttocks and without warning spanked her bottom sharply until the lotion was worked into her warm skin.

She turned over and he moved down to her feet, working his way up her front. He skipped over her breasts and her tight vagina until he had finished every square inch of her skin. Then he plunged into her and made love to her with a fever he had seldom felt before.

Later that afternoon Alan dozed on deck as Sharon went below and got a few items out of the lunch basket. Working quietly she handcuffed him to the boat rail, as he lay on his stomach. He woke up when she poured a bucket of seawater on his backside.

"Sharon! What are you up to?" he demanded.

"I thought you were all too familiar with those hands of yours when you rubbed on my suntan lotion," she told him sternly. "And you had the utter gall to spank me while I was covered with sunscreen. I also don't remember being asked if I wanted to make love. I've decided you need to learn a little discipline."

She poured more cold water over his butt, and then whipped him with a wide hemp rope that she had soaked in seawater. She used it fairly harshly but not with any desire to raise welts. The whipping gave him an erection. After a while he rolled over to show it to her.

"I suppose you think I should take care of that for you." She gestured at his erect penis.

"Well, if you don't mind, my love mistress." He met her eyes with a soft gaze.

"I guess if I caused the erection, I should be the one to take care of it for you," she sighed dramatically before she lowered her mouth to his cock.

"I want to be inside you," he managed to get out before all rational thought fled.

"Next time," she had a glint in her eyes as she raised her mouth just enough to say, "my love, next time."

Chapter Twenty-seven

Betting On Your Future

Christie and Randy cuddled up in bed after their initiation, basking in the afterglow of lovemaking and talking about the club. Christie was idly stroking Randy's chest as they talked and soon, thumbing his nipples without a thought, never even realizing she was doing anything, she began to rub her foot gently up and down his calf.

Randy didn't stand for this careless treatment very long. With a fierce growl, he rolled Christie over onto her back and grasped both of her hands in one of his, holding them up over her head. Directing her, without words, to grip the brass bars at the head of the bed.

"Wait here," he ordered, slipping out of bed. "Do not move, especially your hands."

He returned with a vibrator that he used with intimate intensity and complete thoroughness on every inch of her writhing body. Almost every inch of her body. He avoided the one area of her body that screamed out for the relief and release that he could give her. Finally at long last, he buried the vibrator deep inside her and left it there.

"Don't move, stay right where you are," he ordered sternly, slipping once more from the bed. "I'll show you what you get for teasing me."

She heard a ripping sound and turning her head, saw Randy tearing a sheet into long strips. A thought formed in the back of her head, he wouldn't, or would he?

He would. He did. In a flash she was tied hand and foot to the four-poster bed, the vibrator still in place, whirring gently in her warm pussy and sending shivers throughout her whole body.

"Randy, I can't do anything to you, for you, when I'm tied up like this," she whimpered.

"Yes, you can." He kissed her forehead gently and stroked her hair, his mock anger gone. "You can receive the pleasure I want to give you, the love I want to show you. You're giving me joy by receiving the pleasure. There will be other times for you to pleasure me."

Her only answer was a moan as she lost the power of speech, the power of thought, and only sensation remained. It went on forever; he used his hands, his mouth, and the vibrator on every inch of her lovely body. By the time he was finished both Christie and the sheets were covered with evidence of his passion.

The next morning she woke up feeling wonderful and stiff. Looking over at Randy, she noticed that at least part of him was stiff too. Without bothering to wake him up, she lowered her mouth over his erection, driving him crazy before he even opened his eyes.

"Good morning," he said, sated and content.

"Good morning," she told him with a gleam in her eyes. "Do you have any plans for the day or can we relax in bed?"

"I vote for relaxing," he kissed her deeply, "or at least staying in bed. Somehow, I don't think relaxing will be a big part of it."

They started to play with each other. It was tender and gentle play, with the majority of their lust and passion temporarily abated and the tenderness and love between them in full bloom.

As they cuddled together, Christie asked with studied casualness, "Are we still going to the football game tomorrow?"

"Sure," he looked at her, aware of something in her tone, "unless you have a better idea."

"No. I want to go." She kissed him. "Are we going with Bill and Vicki?"

"Of course." He shot her a sideways glance. "Why are you asking?"

"I was just wondering who opened her big mouth and got us invited to the club," Christie said petulantly. "I'll bet it was Vicki."

"It worked out okay, didn't it?" Randy asked gently. "So why are you mad?"

"I'm not mad, really," Christie said slowly, "it's just that I wish she didn't blab about our personal business so much. If it hadn't worked out okay, I'd arrange a little payback."

"Forget Vicki. We'll explain about respecting confidences tomorrow," Randy said. "And let Bill know she's a blabbermouth."

"And now onto the next order of business," Christie grinned. "Want to have a bet on the football game?"

"If you want to. The usual stakes?" he asked casually.

"I thought just this once we'd make it a blind bet. Winner names the stakes after the game is over, no limits," she suggested, her eyes wide and innocent.

"You have something up your sleeve," he accused. "I've seen that look before. That wide-eyed innocence is an act."

"Randy, my love, I'm naked, remember? No sleeves at all." She looked at him wide-eyed and innocent. "Don't you trust me? Besides, isn't there anything you'd like to have me do? Anything you could name as stakes if you won. Remember, you almost always win. I'm the one taking a real chance here."

"Why do I think that if you win the stakes are going to be astronomical? There's something you really want," Randy relented, "but there's something I really want too. It's a bet. Let's shake on it."

"Forget that." Christie grabbed for him. "I'd rather fuck on it."

They woke early Sunday morning. Randy nuzzled Christie's neck and mumbled, "Are you sure we have to get up? I could just lie here all day."

"I'm sorry, Love, but as hard as it is for me to admit, I have needs that you can't fulfill here in this bed," Christie told him, pushing him away.

"What needs?" Randy said, his voice rising. He reached for her again.

"Right now, a toilet, a toothbrush, a shower and food come to mind." She pushed him away, harder this time, and jumped out of bed running for the bathroom.

"Can I join you in the shower?" Randy called after her when he heard the water running.

"No, my love, you can start breakfast," she mumbled back, talking around her toothbrush. "Put on some coffee. Oh! And there's some of those refrigerator cinnamon rolls in the kitchen. Preheat the oven and put the rolls in a pie tin. Set the timer for 10 minutes and I'll finish breakfast while you shower. I'm hungry!"

While Randy had his shower, Christie made eggs and bacon, set the table and poured the coffee. By the time he got to the table everything was ready. They ate slowly and enjoyed their breakfast before arguing over the Sunday crossword puzzle. Then they took a long walk, hand in hand, before loading up the car with everything they needed for a great tailgate party. They had a barbecue, and some marinated chicken breasts, potato salad, chips and dip, cold beer and fresh apple pie.

So, on the Sunday after their initiation ceremony, Christie and Randy were back at the stadium, side by side with Bill and Vicki. They gently reminded Vicki that even though it turned out alright, she was not required to gossip about them every chance she got. Vicki apologized and things between the friends got back to normal.

As usual they had a bet on the outcome of the game but this time the bet was different, this time the stakes weren't settled in advance. This time the winner could ask for absolutely anything he or she wanted.

Christie wondered to herself if she really had the nerve to ask Randy for what she wanted, what she wanted more than anything in the world.

It didn't matter because as usual Randy won. He had the luck of the devil almost every time they bet on anything. She sighed with disappointment and wondered idly how many of these bets she would lose before she would finally win. Just once.

"So what are you going to ask me for?" she asked him, a little listlessly. "What do you want as your payoff?

"A lot of things." He leered at her and winked. "For starters, you can take me out to dinner, someplace very nice and very expensive. Of course, you can buy. After dinner, I'll tell you what the real payoff is."

Over dinner, Randy asked her, "Christie, what would you have asked me for if you'd won the bet?"

"I'll never tell." She gave him a smile full of mystery and devilment. "I'll just have to win next time. It would have been a heck of a lot more than buying me dinner though, that's for sure."

"I have something more in mind too." Seeing her start to speak, he said quickly, "You'll just have to wait."

She was more than a little disappointed when he suggested they go home after dinner without asking anything more of her. Oh well, she mused, maybe he'll want something special in bed and that can't be bad, it never was.

They made love, and it was tender and sweet. They didn't do anything that could even remotely be considered kinky. They didn't need to; their love and passion was extraordinary.

In the afterglow, when he recovered his breathing enough to talk, Randy said, "Okay, here's the main thing I want as a payoff for the bet. It's a biggie. I want you to marry me, have my kids and grow old with me. Will you?"

"Of course I will." She gazed at him, her eyes full of love and tenderness. "I'd never fail to pay off a bet. It would ruin my reputation."

"Would you tell me now what you wanted, if you had won?" Randy asked. "What was it you were taking such a risk for?"

"I wanted to get married, to have your baby and to spend my life with you," she admitted.

"What do you want to bet the first one's a girl?" Randy laughed as he pulled her towards him again.

"I don't think I'm going to bet anymore." She smiled lovingly up at him. "I'm going to quit while I'm ahead."

"But you lost the bet," he said. "How can you say you're ahead?"

"Did I lose?" She smiled a secret smile that all women have, full of love and mystery. "Somehow, I don't think so."

Chapter Twenty-eight

The Kinky Carnival

Several months after the *Slave Auction* the club members held their First Annual **Spring Carnival**. The carnival was scheduled to be open to the public on Saturday from 9:00 AM until midnight and on Sunday, from 9:00 AM until 9:00 PM, with a private party for adult members only on Friday night, from 10:00 PM until 2:00 AM. Almost all the members were there for the private party.

For the club members' party, they only used a couple of rides. They paid the owner of the carnival quite well for private use of the Ferris wheel and the Merry-go-round, and a few of the booths for the midway games. They also paid him quite a bit to keep the regular carnies far away.

Suzanne hired an off-duty police officer, Robert Wilson, to act as the head of security. She picked him because after the conversation they had at the *Casino Night*, she knew he would be fair and open-minded. Heck, she even knew he would be interested. She had also invited him to bring his wife with him. He also had several of the male club members patrolling with him for backup. The club members were fairly nervous about one thing: They had never held one of their activities outside before, in clear view of the road. Of course, it was a very lightly traveled road, with especially little traffic after dark, but it still was an open road. As usual, that nervousness only served to add greatly to their fun.

The adults rode the Merry-go-round with the sound and lights turned off. After all, even though it was dark, they were outside, and most of them had their pants down. Some of the riders lay across their wooden horses with bare bottoms, others sat on the horses in a normal position. Jerry, Mario and James were stationed around the perimeter with long thin whips, slashing at the riders as they went by. Sometimes they slashed at the rider's legs and sometimes at his or her butt, depending on what they could reach. Mac was different. He was actually stationed on the Merry-go-round, walking with a paddle and using it with a heavy hand on all the bare asses he could reach. Sometimes he would sternly order a rider to rise up off the horse and lean over the wooden neck like a jockey so that he could paddle that rider's butt. The rider always complied.

The police officer, Robert, had brought his wife, Diana, as a specially invited guest. Although she had been told that she was not obligated to try anything, she timidly got into position sitting astride the brightly painted horse. Soon, Mac sternly ordered her to assume the jockey position. She did. She felt awkward and embarrassed with her bottom sticking up in the air. She had decided not to lower her navy blue cotton slacks, but she was up there, riding, ready for Mac to paddle her bottom. The men on the outside held back, not slashing her legs or ass with their whips; they preferred to let Mac with his almost uncanny judgment of how much force to put into his blows, take care of her.

Although she tensed up each time he came near her, Mac only gave her light swats with the paddle the first two times he went by, causing her behind to sting just the tiniest bit. On the third time he came up to her, he noticed that she didn't tense her buttocks when he was near. This time he hit her with a slightly harder force, a really stinging blow, and he held the paddle on her butt for several long moments. She turned her head and looked at him with surprise in her soft brown eyes.

"Gotcha!" he grinned, winking at her.

He reached over and pulled down her slacks revealing her silky mauve underwear and hit her again, a loud, hard cracking swat with the paddle. He gave the nod to the men with the long whips around the perimeter. From that point on, although they were not very harsh with her, she got her share of slashing cuts as she went around. She soon realized that she was genuinely enjoying

205

the light, barely stinging punishment.

Before the Merry-go-round was turned off, Mac had her lean across the horse with her long silky blond hair almost dragging onto the floor on the other side. When she was in position, Mac reached out without a word and slid down her silky underwear. It was not the most comfortable position to be in and she was both scared and embarrassed, but it made it easier and more fun for the men to whip her butt as she went by.

Suzanne, who was walking around and watching all the action, saw Robert standing in the shadows. He had stopped patrolling and was watching with a sly smile as Mac paddled his wife. She quietly went over to the clubhouse and got a paddle.

"Okay, Bud. Drop those pants and bend over. Since you find it so interesting, I've decided that," Suzanne said, sneaking up behind him, "it's time for you to get a taste of the paddle yourself."

"You can't do that; I'm on duty," Robert said grinning and backing away from her.

"I can and I will, or I will call all the members over here," she threatened. "I'm sure as a group they'd be interested in helping make sure you got your just deserts."

"This is assault on an officer of the law," he said, but he was still grinning even as he began to unzip his uniform pants.

"So? Arrest me," Suzanne laughed, "after. Bend over and brace yourself against that tree."

As soon as he bent over and braced himself with his hands against the trunk of the tree, she paddled him. She wasn't especially harsh, just stinging, but she kept it up for about a dozen blows, then she lowered his jockey shorts and gave him another dozen. She finished off with two very harsh blows that left faint bruises.

"I made those last two hard enough to leave bruises deliberately, so you would have some evidence," she said smiling sweetly, "just in case you decided to press those charges."

"Gee, thanks a lot," he said sarcastically, but with a large grin. He rubbed his ass, and pulled up his pants.

"Instead of having her arrested, why don't you just paddle her butt in return." Neither one of them had heard James come up behind them. "It's a lot quicker and a much more satisfying way to get justice."

"Good idea. Suzanne, bend over," Robert commanded. He hit her bare butt a few times with the paddle but not very hard, and left her standing there in the shadows with James.

As he walked away, Robert looked back and saw them sinking to the ground together in a passionate embrace. He went to find Diana.

"Hey, wife," he came up behind her, and kissed her neck, "I wonder if there is anyplace where we can go to be alone around here?"

Sherry, who was walking by, happened to hear him. "Pardon me, but I couldn't help overhearing. I think one of the bedrooms in the clubhouse might be empty. All we ask is that you please just remember to change the sheets when you're done."

She walked away. Robert took Diana's hand and led her into the clubhouse in search of a bedroom.

The club members moved on to the Ferris wheel; no one noticed that a car driving along the usually deserted road had stopped and a couple had gotten out.

They walked through the trees, watching the club members quietly. They were amazed at what they saw, and more than a little worried.

"Dick," Wendy asked quietly, "do you think these people are supposed to be here? Or are they trespassing?"

"They sure act like they belong here," Dick told her, grinning wickedly, "and remember this is supposed to be some sort of private sex club. Just look at all those bare bottoms."

"This is too much," Wendy said as she saw a man pull down a woman's pants and spank her bare bottom soundly. "Wow!"

"Come on girl," he teased her. "I know you've had a few sexual spankings, remember? It was my hand giving them to you."

"I know how it feels to beat your butt too, mister, and don't you forget it," she shot back. "But we never did it in public or as

207

part of a group."

"Or outdoors," he added dryly.

"Let's get out of here for now before we're seen," Wendy urged. "But let's come to the fair tomorrow." They didn't know that James saw them get into their car and go.

At the Ferris wheel it was waiting in line that was the punishment. The riders each had long, thin whips. As they descended, they slashed at the bare butts of the people bending over, waiting for their turn to get on.

The first riders had to wait at the end of the line to give the last riders some targets. Sarah was put in charge of lining up the people who were waiting, and positioning them properly so that they could be whipped by the riders without being hit by the Ferris wheel itself. The line was slowed down by the fact that she kept checking on the positions by putting herself in place for the descending whips. Finally, Clayton grabbed a paddle and beat her severely.

"Thanks Clay, I needed that," she told him.

"Anytime, Sarah." He kissed her cheek. "You are a greedy little thing, aren't you?"

She gave him a wide-eyed look, innocence shining in her bright green eyes. "Who, me?"

"Now be a good little girl, or I'll make sure that none of us ever spanks you again," he threatened sternly. The line moved along at a steady pace after a terrible threat like that.

The bell striker was set up so that anyone who failed to ring the gong got swats with a paddle, depending on how badly they missed it. Clay had volunteered to handle the game. On the other side of the carnival grounds, players got paid with spankings when their numbers came up on the brightly painted wheel of fortune. Mario was in charge of that duty. Sherry turned out to be his biggest customer. They had a dunk tank, run by Annie and her husband Don, with a three swat reward for anybody scoring a 'dunk.'

There was also a swatting booth, run by Jerry and Edna. Jerry took the women over his knee spanking them with his bare hand, while Edna used a paddle on the men. Her first customer was James.

"Hey, sweetheart," he said, kissing her cheek, "how about a long hard one? Can you make it hurt so good?"

"For you, James my love, I can make it hurt so bad," she replied with her usual sweet smile.

James got into the traditional position. "Okay sweetie, make it good."

And she certainly did. James left to find his wife once again. He didn't have far to go since she was in line in front of Jerry. James waited for her to get to the front of the line and watched her get her spanking and then grabbed her hand, pulling her away.

"Let's go find a bedroom," he said with a wicked grin.

"Again?" Suzanne laughed. "What am I going to do with you?"

"When we find an empty bed, I'll show you," he answered, laughing. "Gladly."

Toni watched them from her position in line. She took her turn, getting a harsh spanking from Jerry, and then she went in search of her husband. When she found him, she persuaded him to shut down the wheel of fortune game and join her on one of the Merry-go-round horses. It was turned off and very dark with no lights on. They chose the horse that was the most hidden in the shadows and got on it together. They found out that a wooden horse, with a pole and straps for the kids, wasn't nearly as comfortable as a real horse. But there was one advantage. This horse, unlike their big sorrel gelding, didn't buck them off at a crucial moment.

Saturday and Sunday, the carnival was open to the public all day. Most of the married members brought their kids to the fair early on Saturday morning. They strolled around trying to win prizes in the games, and carried the stuffed animals and other prizes the rest of the day. They went on all the rides: the Ferris wheel, Merry-go-round and the roller coaster rides. The dunk tank was a big success. It was strange to see the carnival as a regular place to bring the kids after their sexual games of the night before.

At one point during the day James recognized the couple he had seen walking towards their car the night before. He walked over to introduce himself and to find out what they had been doing there the night before.

"Hi, I'm James." He held out a hand. "I thought I saw you two here last night and I figured you might have some questions or comments about what you saw."

"I'm Dick and this is my wife Wendy," he shook hands with James, "and yes, we were here last night. We weren't spying. We were just driving by and saw people on some of the rides. At first we thought some kids might be playing around or even vandalizing the rides, so we got out of our car to walk over and take a look."

"Frankly, we were um, intrigued by what we saw," Wendy added. "But we left as soon as we realized that it was adults and not teenagers playing around. We didn't want to be rude, and your club has a reputation for guarding its privacy pretty closely."

"We do try to be private, but we're not really fanatical about it. We just don't think our club is for everyone," James told her, smiling. "You could have walked over and joined us if you wanted to."

"If we had been invited we probably would have joined in, but we're not used to walking into a place where we're not sure what our reception would be," Dick told him, then added, "but it looked like fun. Your members certainly were having a real good time."

"Do you two?" James let the question trail off.

"Sometimes," Wendy admitted with a blush.

"Then let me issue an open invitation for you to come visit us in the future." James saw Suzanne and waved her over. "Let me introduce my wife Suzanne and our twin daughters, Mary and Lizzie. Suzanne, these are the people I saw last night, Wendy and her husband Dick. They might be interested in visiting the club in the future."

"How nice. We have a really great group of people, and we're always ready to welcome more." Suzanne smiled at the pair.

"We have to go, we're on the planning committee," James explained. "Have fun at the fair and come visit us soon."

"If you give me your phone numbers, I'll call you when we have time to talk so I can tell you all about the club and see if you'd really want to come to a party or a private event." Suzanne fished in her large purse for a scrap of paper and a pencil.

The rest of the day passed uneventfully. The club had a spaghetti dinner at the clubhouse on Saturday night from 5:00 to 8:00 PM, complete with garlic bread and salads. It was a success, but the carnie food stands did even better. The most popular treat was the cotton candy, followed by hot dogs, popcorn and pizza slices washed down with gallons of soda. Sure enough by the middle of the afternoon, long before the spaghetti dinner, all the members were dragging tired, cranky and slightly queasy kids home for a nap.

When it was over, the members all pitched in to clean up quickly and get the kitchen clean and ready for Sunday's pancake breakfast. Jesse and Janine directed the cleaning. By 9:00 PM all the members went home to put the kids and themselves to bed. The only people who stayed later were the carnies and the non-members. On Saturday night there was very little fooling around in any of the members' beds. They were too tired to bother, a very unusual state for the club members.

The pancake breakfast was held in the clubhouse from 8:00 to 10:00 AM on Sunday. It was a huge success, and this time Jesse had supplied a regular cleaning crew. On Sunday night, although many members brought their kids back to the carnival, they seemed to be in better shape. For one thing, the kids didn't to want to stay so long. For another, they didn't have a spaghetti dinner to fix Sunday night. They also didn't have to work so hard to clean up. Jesse had a crew come back Monday morning and take care of everything. The clubhouse glowed when they were done.

After the carnival most of the members got home early Sunday night. Some of them even managed to relax before bed. In fact, most of the members were refreshed enough to play Sunday night. There were a lot of warm bottoms that night, and lots of sex. Some had it more than once, a few more than twice. Like the old saying, it's hard to keep a good member down.

Chapter Twenty-nine

Initiations, For The Last Time

Suzanne was, as usual, nervous while she was dressing for the Paddle Club initiation. She always was when acting as the hostess because she always wanted the prospective members to have a good time. This time there were two couples interested in joining.

She had talked to each of the couples, both as a pair and to each person individually. She had very comfortable feelings about these people. They all seemed very congenial, friendly and sexy. Unlike her club initiation, all these people seemed to understand exactly what they were getting into.

Remembering her own initiation always made her smile. She had been so scared, and her boyfriend Michael had been such a jerk. That night she met James and dumped Michael for good. After five years they were still deeply in love, and still very active and involved in the Paddle Club.

James came into the bedroom. He walked up behind her and slid his hands around her waist, stroking the soft swell of her belly.

"How's the little guy tonight?" he asked her solicitously.

"The little guy's just hanging in there. He should start kicking soon. Do you really want a boy this time?" She turned to smile up at him.

"Well, we do have twin girls. But no, not really, I just want a healthy baby. Take it easy tonight, okay?" He kissed her tenderly.

"You know I will." She kissed him back. "As long as that wicked witch of the west, Nancy, keeps her mitts off your body I will. But if she touches you one more time I swear I'll snatch her bald."

"She's really a pleasant girl," James offered, with feigned innocence. "She's just flirting."

"She's a bitch who's permanently in heat, and she's been after you since the day she joined the club." She hugged him. "Don't get me wrong, I trust you, but that bitch gets my goat."

"Okay, okay. What a mixed metaphor. I'll stay as far away from her as I can. But if you actually attack her, I'll beat you senseless," he threatened. "After you have that baby." As he turned away, she slapped him as hard as she could on his ass.

"I'll get you for that!" he yelled playfully.

"I'll make a note of it. Let's see," she pretended to write in a notebook, "James promises to get revenge in… " she thought, "the baby's due in May, so maybe the end of June? I'll start quaking in my boots later."

"You do that." James took her in his arms and kissed her, a long hard and passionate kiss.

"How much time do we have?" Suzanne asked.

"Enough." James reached for the zipper of her long, red silk dress.

Just then, they heard the doorbell ring. It was Janie, the babysitter. James heaved a long and dramatic sigh and put on a long-suffering air as he went to greet her while Suzanne finished dressing.

"Hi Janie, Suzanne's just getting dressed." He smiled at her. "How have you been?"

"I've got a new boyfriend named Bobby, if that tells you anything. He's really, really nice. He treats me as if I'm the most precious thing in the world," she told James proudly.

"Good girl. If he cares for you then you are the most precious person in the world." James hugged her. "How's college?"

"I'm doing okay, 3.4 average, but it's very hard." She grinned at him. "It cuts into the time I could spend with my boyfriend."

"I remember the feeling." He smiled.

"Oh really?" She looked at him wide-eyed, with feigned innocence. "When you were in college, you had a boyfriend too?"

James grabbed the girl and wrestled her to the floor mindless of his good tuxedo, and began to tickle her without mercy.

"Ahem!" Suzanne cleared her throat. "James, my love, if you're through rolling on the floor with the babysitter, we have to be leaving. I'm the hostess tonight, remember?"

The pair jumped up so fast that an outside observer would have thought the carpet was on fire. "Suzanne! We were just, um... "

"I know, I stood there just watching for a few minutes," she laughed. "The guilty looks on your faces, and the way you jumped up off the floor. God! It was so funny. But we really do have to leave."

"Hold down the fort, Janie. Call Bobby if you finish your homework." James waved as he went for the door, then turned back to the girl. "But if I catch him here before you get that homework done, I'll spank you both. And tell him yes," Janie's eyes widened with shock before James finished, "you do really have to wear a bathing suit in the pool."

"Goodnight you two, have, um... fun." Janie followed them to the door and watched them leave before settling down on the sofa with her Calculus homework.

When James and Suzanne got to the club she made her usual check of the arrangements, and greeted Jerry before joining James in the main room.

There was a little business before the new members arrived. The main topic of concern was that their clubhouse, which had been quite a distance outside the city limits when they had built it, would soon be very close to the town. The city was spreading out. They also wanted to become more a part of the community, and with so many new young couples joining lately, they wanted to have more public and family events, such as barbecues and dances.

Of course they planned on continuing the monthly parties, along with special events like the *Slave Auction*, *Maze* and the *Casino Night*. They decided however, to make the *Carnival* a strictly legitimate event. They also discussed the club's plan for a cruise again.

They also decided to purchase some of the open land next to the clubhouse to build a park and a large parking lot. There were about twenty acres up for sale. That way they could donate the use of the park to the city, complete with a few tennis and basketball courts, a large swimming pool and a baseball diamond. They would also have walking and biking paths and an area for cookouts. It would boost their public image, increase their community involvement, and still give them the privacy to continue their spanky games. All those benefits, plus it would be good for the community and provide a great tax write-off for the club.

Clayton said it best. "It's a win, win situation. And we've always said that our spanking games are only a small portion of our total sexual identities so why should that be the only thing we have in common? Why can't we be involved in our community as well? It won't take anything away from our enjoyment, it should only add to it."

Shortly after Clayton made his speech, the project was voted on and overwhelmingly approved by the general membership. They were still having discussions about it as the prospective members arrived.

Suzanne studied the couples as she made her introductions to the club members. She liked to find a distinguishing characteristic for each new member, to help her remember who was who. The first couple was a pair named Wendy and Dick. Wendy had short black hair and brown eyes. Although she was busty, there was an innocent air about her. Her husband Dick was blond, with neatly trimmed hair and mustache. His most notable characteristic was his devotion to his wife.

The other new pair was the handsome police officer, Robert and his wife Diana. Diana had long, silky blond hair and a great shape. She seemed to be a gentle, intelligent lady. Robert was the type of man who sounded plain when he was described: brown hair and brown eyes, with a medium build. This description was extremely deceiving; he was a man who would always be described by women as a hunk. She led them to the special chairs on the dais and had them be seated. Then she called the party to order.

As in her own initiation, they started off by letting the prospective members use the canes to whip any of the members who wanted a whipping. With four new members, the whippings took a long time and several of the old members had been whipped more than once before it was over. A few diehards even went whole hog and had whippings from all four of the prospective members. Those members were called 'leather butts' by some of the others.

Then there was a long pause for a round of drinks and some socializing before it was the new members' turn to be whipped into the club.

First it was Wendy's turn to be strapped down and severely whipped by the club members. Wendy was in her mid-twenties with short, wavy black hair and brown eyes. She was slender, yet still large busted. Suzanne picked Wendy first because she was the most nervous. Suzanne knew she would get even more terrified if she had to wait and watch the others.

In spite of her fear, Wendy took her whipping well. Her husband, Dick, took his well too. Only his dark brown eyes reflected any of his pain or discomfort during his whipping. Suzanne knew from private conversations with Wendy that she and Dick spanked each other occasionally as part of their sex lives. It all started with a birthday spanking on the first night they made love. What Suzanne didn't know was that it was also the night Wendy lost her virginity and became engaged to Dick. It had been quite a night!

Diana took her whipping well and even made a remark that it hurt a lot less than a traffic fine. A remark that some of the members didn't quite understand. Robert also took his whipping well; he even seemed to relax and enjoy it up to a point. Unfortunately, that point was about the halfway point. All the couples were accepted for membership. The party started to break up and most of the members drifted off.

Mac grabbed Sarah and dragged her off to one of the

bedrooms. "Come here little girl, I have something to show you," he said, taking her hand and placing it on the straining fly of his tight jeans.

"I've already seen it," Sarah said, looking into his bright blue eyes. "Besides, my mother told me to avoid men like you."

"But that was when you were just a little girl," he told her, nuzzling her ear.

"No, actually it was last week," she informed him. She kissed him with passion. "Mac, let's go home. If we stay here we have to get up in a few minutes and change the sheets. If we go home we can stay there and play all night long."

"With champagne and photos?" he asked.

"Why don't we test out the new video camera?" Sarah suggested. "I feel like a movie star."

"You have a wicked mind, my love." Mac kissed her and patted her fanny. "Let's go home and I'll reward you for it."

Jerry and Edna helped Jesse and Janine clean up for a while, then made their excuses and left.

As Jerry put it, "We'd better get home. I have to make love to this hot number all night long," he hugged Edna close, "and still get up early enough to take a couple of my grandkids fishing."

"We're getting old, dear," Edna told him.

"I'll spank you for that remark," he smiled as he threatened her.

"Promises, promises," she said sweetly, humor flashing in her merry brown eyes.

Hearing that, Mario and Toni said they had to leave too. "We're competing in a horse show in the morning. We have to leave the stables by 7:00 AM to be there on time," Toni explained.

"That means getting up by six to get dressed, eat and hitch up the trailer," Mario added.

"That reminds me, Honey, is all the tack packed and loaded in the trailer already?" Toni asked.

"It should be; the saddles, bridles and brushes are in the trailer. So are the spurs and some feed for the horses." Mario paused thinking. "Oh man, I almost forgot one thing."

"What?" Toni asked.

"My riding crop is in the bedroom." Mario almost blushed.

The whole group laughed at that, but not as hard as when James asked casually, "Have you been riding the horses in the house again, Mario? Or did the crop get there some other way?"

"What are your plans for the weekend, Dick?" James asked casually.

"Wendy and I are going up to our cabin in the mountains to play in the snow."

"There's something about cold snow piled onto hot red buns that's really, ah, exhilarating," Wendy added innocently.

"Snow?" James said intrigued. "Sounds fun."

"How about you?" Suzanne asked Robert.

"Well, compared to everyone else's plans this probably sounds boring, but whenever one of us has shall we say, a sore butt, we comfort each other with pizza and cold beer," Robert admitted.

"And of course, good hot sex," Diane added.

"Works for me," James agreed. "Suzanne and I just go home and fool around, and play with the kids."

"We're just plain old married folks," Suzanne laughed, "with whips and chains."

"What chains?" James asked, laughing.

When everyone else had left except Clayton and Sherry, James came up behind to Suzanne. Although everything had already been well taken care of by Jesse, she was straightening things up. He swatted her butt. "Hey, I've heard about another couple that might be interested in joining our little group," he told her. "Their names are Martin and Sandy."

"Who recommended them?" Suzanne asked.

"Clayton," James answered. "It seems like there was a whipping involved in bringing them together as a couple, but Clayton claims he doesn't know the whole story. He said Martin's boss might even be interested."

"Have Clayton give them our number and they can call me if they're interested. I bet I can get the whole story." Suzanne kissed her husband.

"You, my love, could get the whole story from a Russian spy."

James returned her kiss.

Forgetting all about the other couple in the building, she dragged James down to her on the loveseat.

Sherry stuck her head out of the kitchen door. She turned to Clayton and said, "They're at it again. Let's go into one of the bedrooms."

He lifted her onto the kitchen counter and said, "Why go to all that trouble?" Slowly he lowered the zipper on his fly.

James slid Suzanne's underwear and hose off her long, silky legs. She sat up and pulled her dress over her head while James undressed. James lay down beside her on the soft loveseat.

Suzanne told him, "I think I fell in love with you that first night when I was on this loveseat after my whipping, and you were so kind to me."

"I fell in love with you then too. I fell in love with your courage, humor and looks, and even your serenity." James leaned over his wife and kissed her passionately. Then he admitted, "I'm always a little scared at these initiations, that maybe you'll fall in love again. Just like you did when you were the one being initiated."

"I do fall in love again at every initiation but only with you, my darling, only with you. What do I need with another man?" She kissed him intimately, taking his long cock into her mouth. Then she raised her head, "I already have a man who can light a fire in my heart," another intimate kiss, "and on my butt." James rolled her over and slid into her.

Author's Note

Some of the couples in this book are not given their full history because each couple already has their own story in another pair of books. These books contain a series of short stories, and some of them feature club members. The books are called *Hot Crossed Buns* and *Another Batch of Hot Buns*.

Among the stories you'll find:

→ Sarah & Mac in *Store Bought Pain*
→ Robert & Diana in *C.O.P.S. – Count On Painful Smacks*
→ Wendy & Dick in *Tender Lovemaking*
→ Christie & Randy in *You Bet Your Ass*
→ Sandy & Martin in *Office Pranks, Office Spanks*
→ Jesse and Janine in *Jesse The Hard-Handed Janitor*

I hope you'll enjoy reading their stories. Thank you.

Susan Kohler

www.ingramcontent.com/pod-product-compliance
Lightning Source LLC
Chambersburg PA
CBHW020838260626
47169CB00003B/1041